D0090604

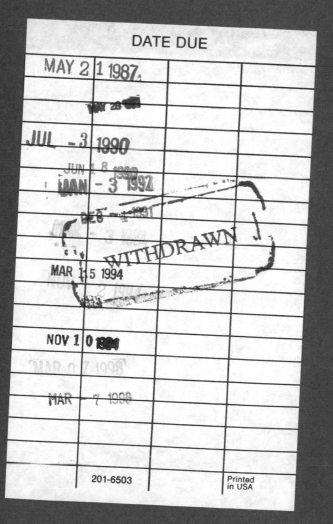

THE OSTRICH CHASE

Moses L. Howard

THE OSTRICH CHASE

Illustrated
by Barbara Seuling

Holt, Rinehart and Winston
New York   Chicago   San Francisco

Library of Congress Cataloging in Publication Data

Howard, Moses L
The ostrich chase.

SUMMARY: Although the women are forbidden to
participate in the hunt, a young Bushman girl
determines to realize her dream of hunting an
ostrich.
[1. Bushmen—Fiction. 2. Kalahari Desert—
Fiction] I. Seuling, Barbara, illus. II. Title.
PZ7.H8340s   [Fic]   73–17372
ISBN 0–03–012096–9

Printed in the United States of America: 074

Designed by Sandra Kandrac
First Edition

To My Daughter, Bonnie

Contents

1

The Bushmen Camp

It was late afternoon and the hot sand of the Kalahari desert burned into Khuana's feet. The hot sand made her run faster, because it pushed up through her toes and gave way under her feet as she ran. The searing sun beat down on her young body, sending rivulets of sweat down her copper-colored skin. She looked back anxiously over her shoulder to see if anyone was watching her. No one moved in the camp. As she ran on, a sand dune blotted the camp from her sight and she thought of nothing but her errand.

Khuana heard voices ahead and slowed down; then bending down, she crept forward. The beads strung in her hair clinked against the copper bracelets on her arm as she pulled a desert bush aside and peered down into a dried-out riverbed. The men were there, just as she knew they would be. They had already started their work, but they had not begun what she had come to watch. She congratulated herself on being in time for the important part. No air moved around Khuana's face. Her throat felt parched and dry and her nose seemed too narrow to take in the air she needed. As she wiped sweat from her forehead with the back of her arm, the few parched leaves on the bush crackled so loudly that Khuana thought the men would hear her and look up from their work.

Overhead, the sky was blue with only a few puffs of white cloud. Sometimes, lone birds could be seen soaring above, but on this day nothing moved. The sun's heat rippled up from the sand and the men kept in a close circle in the shadow cast by a thorn tree. In the circle in front of them were their weapons. Khuana could see them from where she knelt behind the bush; bows and arrows, quivers, short spears, and clubs. She could hear the snapping and twanging of bow strings, the sharpening of arrowheads on stones and the dull grating sound of wood on leather as they firmly pressed arrows into quivers.

This was not the first time Khuana had watched the men; she watched whenever she had the chance to slip away from helping her mother. While Khuana watched, she kept glancing over her shoulder to see if any of the camp women were about. She had found out at a very early age it was bad for a girl to show interest in arrows, bows, or any other hunting tools—they were "men's things." She stared hard at the men. She wanted to see if they were putting poison on their arrows for hunting. She almost forgot the heat of the desert sand as she pressed one knee down onto it. She was so intent on watching that she did not hear the soft sound of feet upon sand behind her.

"So!" The scratching voice of an old woman frightened

2

her and she almost jumped straight up. She turned around to face old Mrs. Samgau who had crept up behind her. The old woman squinted at her, pointing a shaking, bony finger.

"I'll tell the other women," she threatened. "You know these are men's things."

Khuana looked around nervously to see if the men had heard. It was one thing to be discovered by the women, but far worse if the men knew. Khuana kept a respectful silence while old Mrs. Samgau went on in the same grating voice.

"You are always wishing you were a boy—forgetting how to dig roots, but thinking you can hunt big animals."

She hoped the old woman would soon tire of scolding her and order her away.

"You'll get into trouble. I *always* said so." The old crone held a tobacco leaf which she sniffed from time to time.

Khuana began moving away as the old woman came closer.

"Now, go and help your mother with the food gathering," she suddenly shouted. Khuana turned and ran as fast as she could, the sand flying up behind her. She didn't look back until she was sure she had left old Mrs. Samgau far behind.

As she approached the camp a small figure jumped out from behind a skerm, caught her by the legs, and sent Khuana tumbling over into the sand. At first she was frightened. Had old Mrs. Samgau caught her? When she looked up she saw her young brother, Gishay, running away across the sand and looking back laughing at her. "That Gishay!" she said aloud, picking up a handful of

3

sand and feeling its heat run through her fingers. "Ouch, the desert eye is angry today," she said, glancing at the sun.

She was too exhausted to chase Gishay and fell back on the ground, feeling the hot sand as it clung to her sweaty face and neck. That silly, naughty Gishay, she thought. Then her brown face broke into a smile—after all, better Gishay than old Mrs. Samgau, she thought.

She lay there only a short while before she felt a hand shaking her.

"What's wrong Khuana, do you want to get sun fever?"

Khuana started—then smiled up at the girl. "Oh, Nsue, you are the third person to frighten me. I thought you were old Mrs. Samgau."

The girl was one dry season older that Khuana. Her body was rounder, her face smoother. She wore a band of plaited ostrich-shell beads around her forehead, and her body, which smelled of the scent of the Sjaae bush— the powder of the bush women—was as smooth as butter. Khuana looked at her friend. They had been together almost all their lives. Khuana loved her more than all the other girls and she felt Nsue loved her too. Yet there was one great difference between them. Nsue was everything a Bushman mother wanted her daughter to be, but Khuana did not often meet the approval of her mother or any of the Bushmen women.

"I am glad you are not old Mrs. Samgau," Khuana breathed with relief.

Nsue laughed. "Why should I be?" Then she went on, "I saw her a little while ago. She's out hunting wild tobacco. What's wrong?"

"Come on, let's go to my mother's skerm," Khuana

4

said, pulling herself up by the hand Nsue gave her. "I want to be there when she tells mother."

"Who? Tell your mother what?"

"She caught me watching the men prepare for the hunt."

"Oh, Khuana!" said Nsue, in disappointment. "You didn't! Won't you ever give up this silly idea? Everybody knows weapons are for men. They would never let a mere girl go hunting, so why do you keep trying?"

"Nsue, I do so wish I could hunt like other people do. Boys can do whatever they want; why shouldn't we do the same?"

Nsue shook her head with impatience. "Khuana, you talk as though you'd been eating bitter melons. Are you ill?"

"Yes! I mean no, I'm not sick. But, yes, oh yes, I do want to hunt. Not a chamois, not the toughest animals hunted by men, but ostriches."

"Ostriches! Those things are dangerous." Nsue's eyes widened. "A chamois will at least run away from you, but if an ostrich is guarding eggs, it may kill you with its beak or sharp toes."

They walked on in silence.

"Old Mrs. Samgau will be coming any time," Khuana looked over her shoulder. "She's going to tell the women —mother will be so ashamed."

"Don't worry, everyone knows what a grumbler old Mrs. Samgau is," said Nsue. Then she continued more tenderly, "Still, Khuana, we must remember the trouble she has had."

"I am only thinking about my poor grandmother. She will be so disappointed in me."

5

The two girls, holding hands, passed by the hurriedly built skerms. These skerms often consisted of no more than three or four sticks pushed into the loose sand, bent over and covered with grass and bush to keep out the searing Kalahari sun. The camp lay in a little hollow surrounded by a few thorn trees, sparse bush, and grass. The parched brown grass stood mute, for there was no wind to stir the hot breath of the desert.

"Khuana, you always speak of hunting your silly long-necked ostriches," Nsue said, after some time. "But I would love to be where there is nothing but Sjaae grass growing. I would grind it into sweet perfumed powder to keep in my tortoiseshell powder box."

"Nsue! I want all those things too—sweet-smelling powders, scented oil from the white lace tree, and the tortoiseshell powder box my grandmother has promised me. Nsue, can't you see I like beads in my hair?" she said, fingering her beads.

"Then why is it you can only speak of ostriches?"

Khuana could not remember when she first wanted to hunt an ostrich. Perhaps it was when she first sat by the evening fires listening to Cripple Guike, the Bushman storyteller, telling stories about the beauty and the swiftness of the ostrich. She had seen, almost real, an image of ostriches striding across the desert, raising and lowering their heads. But she also wanted to hunt them because their eggs were useful. She knew the importance of carrying water in ostrich eggshells. A person with an eggshell full of water was never thirsty on a journey in the desert. Besides, beads and buttons made from eggshells were very lovely. Many useful things came from the ostrich. She considered it a beautiful and useful bird. She was aware of its beauty, and, vaguely, she was also aware of its danger, and so hunting it was the supreme challenge for her. When Cripple Guike told of the swiftness, the stealth, and the accuracy a hunter must have, Khuana sometimes saw herself tracking the gemsbok or the wary chamois; but always, at the back of her mind, the ostrich was her prize.

From the first she had wondered why boys should do all the best things. She wanted ostrich-shell beads, so why shouldn't she shoot an ostrich? She could hunt and find an ostrich egg just as well as her brother Gishay. Why should she wait for her father to bring an ostrich egg for her grandmother to decorate and make into a canteen? Khuana could not accept the women's warnings to keep away from "men's things." So she made plans of her own and watched the men and boys at work on their weapons and tried to learn as much as possible.

Soon after Khuana and Nsue arrived back in camp, the people heard a loud "Morro, Morro." Everyone stared out onto the desert from where the sound seemed to come, and soon Cripple Guike appeared as if out of a sand dune, running in his crippled hip-hop manner, sweat pouring off his body.

He ran on until he collapsed at old Tsona's feet. Khuana and Nsue were just behind old Tsona and saw Cripple Guike's tongue hanging from the side of his mouth, his eyes rolling in his head.

"What is it?" asked old Tsona, kneeling beside him.

"Is he hurt?" Khuana asked. Cripple Guike could not speak. His tongue lolled out of the corner of his mouth.

His lips, completely dry, opened but no sound came from them. But he kept looking towards the desert. Khuana heard wise old Tsona say to her father standing nearby: "He's probably seen meat and run too fast. Now he must rest before he can tell us."

The people followed his eyes to the desert, but saw nothing. Old Tsona called for water. He propped up Cripple Guike's head and poured water from a small gourd cup. He poured the water slowly. Guike swallowed hard between gasps for air, and his face showed his thankfulness. After a while he was able to whisper: "Chamois there; giant chamois."

"He's seen a chamois," said old Tsona to the people. Then to Guike, he said, gently, "Not so fast. Don't try to talk too quickly."

After several attempts the story came out. Cripple Guike had sighted a giant chamois less than half a day away. He had been out scouting for food and inspecting a water hole. The water hole was dried up—there was only water at Guatscha pan, some twenty miles away in the foothills that led to mountains far away west. He had found no water, but while returning had seen the chamois. He was very excited and had wanted to follow it and shoot it there and then, but realized that he would not be able to carry even a quarter of the meat by himself. Then, not wanting to lose the animal, he had run across the hot desert for half a day. The sun and thirst had nearly killed him.

A wave of excitement went through the Bushman camp, for they hoped there would be meat, and the water from the animal's stomach might last them for a few days. The camp water hole was small and almost dry.

Cripple Guike had run as fast as he could to give the men time to get their weapons ready and to dance to Gao Na, their god, to bless the hunt.

Soon after sundown, Khuana and Nsue were in Nsue's mother's skerm when they heard Tsona tell the men to prepare their weapons. Khuana jumped for joy. Tonight was the night! She would get her chance to see the men prepare everything for hunting. She forgot about old Mrs. Samgau who, in the excitement following Guike's return, had forgotten to report Khuana to the women. The two friends laughed at this until they could not stand any longer and fell down onto the sand.

Khuana jumped out of the skerm calling to Nsue to join her, as she clapped her hands and began to dance. Nsue was caught by the rhythm, and facing each other, the two friends strutted forward, hands on their waists, and then arms straight out; they bent double from the hips and pretended they were ostriches. Nsue craned her pretty neck like an ostrich, while Khuana gave a good imitation of the roar of the ostrich. They made a beautiful sight as they speeded up their dance, and then they began to "hissss" and "hiiii" like ostriches playing across the sand.

"Goodness me!" exclaimed old Mrs. Samgau coming up behind them. "Nsue, Khuana! Are you deaf? Guike says it is a chamois."

"Yes," Khuana said, bowing to the rhythm, the beads dancing in her hair.

"But that's an ostrich dance," the old woman said. "That's an ostrich dance or *I'm* an ostrich."

9

2

Poisoned Arrows

Khuana could hardly wait until dark. This time she arrived at the place before the men and she took up a good position where two rocks leaned against each other. She felt their smoothness, rubbing her hands where the sand of many sandstorms had worn an even surface. As soon as the men arrived they started to work on the arrows. Her father, Kwi, put a quiver full of arrows down against a bush whose roots divided again and again to spread across the soil like a giant spider's web. Old Tsona put down his bag beside the quiver of arrows and Khuana quickly ducked down to keep the men from seeing her. It was hard to believe that she was really about to see it. Her eyes widened and her tongue pressed against her teeth. The arrows were hollow reeds tipped with sharply pointed bone. The rounded ends of the bone tips were shaped to fit into the reeds. It was old Tsona's bag that really excited her. The Bushmen used poisoned arrows. In this bag were the beetles that gave the poison which made the Bushmen arrows dangerous to both people and animals.

Old Tsona had told her: "The arrows are not feathered like the ends of the arrows of Zulus and other tribes, so that their accuracy is not good over a long distance. Still, when we stalk, we shoot from a short distance. The underside of the head of the arrow is poisoned, so never touch it."

She knew that once an animal had been shot it ran on. It brushed against bushes, trying desperately to rid itself of the arrow, but when this happened, only the hollow reed came off, leaving the poisoned arrow in the flesh.

Goa came bringing wood in his arms. While he laid a fire, and lighted it with a burning branch from the main fire, Tsona and Kwi got ready. They laid out the arrows and then began taking out the black cocoons that held the poisonous pupae.

The desert night grew chilly and Khuana shivered. She wished she had brought a large chamois skin or her mother's gemsbok cape. But then someone would have seen her and demanded to know where she was going, for at night women seldom visit. She looked toward the campfire. She wondered if they had missed her yet and became worried. Anyway, her old grandmother, Gaushe, knew where she was. Gaushe always knew.

Watching the men, Khuana found that there were two ways to poison the arrows. Kwi's way was faster. He simply broke open the brittle black cocoon with the tip of an arrow, crushed the pupa, and rubbed the poisonous body back and forth along the arrow shaft; the body gleamed silvery white between his fingers as his hand moved up and down the arrowhead.

11

Tsona rebuked Khuana's father, Kwi, for putting poison on the arrows this way. But Tsona rebuked him gently, because, although he was headman of this band and had more age and wisdom, it did not give him the right to be discourteous to any member of the group.

"That's as dangerous as crossing the desert without water," Tsona said.

"I know, but it's faster," Kwi replied.

"The first sleep on the desert is fast, but the second without water is impossible," Tsona pursued the issue. Both men knew exactly what the other would say, it seemed to Khuana, but somehow that didn't stop them from carrying on the dialogue. Tsona had the duty to speak to her father with his wisdom, and her father was bound to defend his position.

"Why do we look over our hands carefully before we begin?" old Tsona asked as if he didn't know.

"So we can see there are no cuts and the skin is not broken."

"If a drop of this gets under the skin, our forefathers will greet you before we sleep twice if it is not sucked out well. It's far better to do it my way and be safe."

Khuana watched Tsona take from the bag a small hollow stone and pestle, and a small stone knife. Old Goa piled more wood on the fire and the sparks whirled in the slow desert air. The dried branches crackled and shadows played on the faces of the three men as they worked. Voices from the camp drifted down into the riverbed. Women laughed and babies cried in the camp. Khuana's eyes watched the deft movements of old Tsona's hands as he opened several of the round, brittle cocoons with his stone knife. The cocoons were dry and his knife made a crunching sound as it prized open the covering. He dropped the silvery shiny bodies into the small stone mortar and ground down the pestle with quick twists of his wrist. At last he held up the pestle, dripping juice, over the mortar. Then he began. Even Kwi's hands stopped work and his eyes showed admiration as old Tsona began squeezing drops of the poison onto the backs of the tips of the arrows. Even my father knows Tsona is wise, thought Khuana.

Old Goa dried the poisoned arrows over the fire and carefully slipped them back into the quivers. After Khuana had watched it all from her place between the two rocks, she slipped away unobserved by anyone. But her grandmother met her as she hurried back. Gaushe was near the foul-smelling water hole getting a drink of water before going to bed. She saw Khuana as she came running by, looking back over her shoulder. Gaushe's voice startled her.

"Running home after doing mischief, are you?"

"Oh!" Khuana started.

The voice was gentle but unexpected.

"It's you, my long mother."

"You should be glad it's no one else."

Khuana rushed to hug her grandmother, Gaushe. Khuana's head came up between the wrinkled, sagging breasts of the old woman. She felt the wrinkled warm skin and the strong beat of the heart against the ribs. With her coils of hair buried between Gaushe's breasts, Khuana imagined the merry smiling eyes that always went with her gentle voice.

"I love you, long mother," Khuana said.

"Long mother loves you and wishes you would give up your silly plans and behave like a girl."

Khuana looked up at Gaushe. "But you promised you'd help me."

"I said I'd help you find a marula tree."

"And if there are no poisonous beetles in the earth beneath it?"

"We'll find another," old Gaushe smiled. "Women are allowed to find the beetles for poisoning arrows. But the rule is that no woman must have anything to do with arrows or hunting weapons. It will bring bad luck to the hunter or his family. Do you want our family to have bad luck?"

"But old Tsona, our headman and the wisest of us all, taught me to shoot the arrow."

"That was different, Khuana. It was just a child's toy," said Gaushe.

"But long mother," Khuana appealed, "did you never want to do things that the men do?"

"I did, and once I shot a small deer."

Khuana jumped for joy in the sand. "You did! Please tell me about it, long mother."

"I'll tell you another time. Now we must go to bed."

They walked back to camp where the fire still blazed, but the talk had stopped and soon everyone was covered with animal skins and breathing rhythmically in sleep. Soon Khuana and her grandmother were also asleep.

The next morning Khuana was first awake in the camp. It was not yet dawn but she could see the first paleness on the eastern horizon. It was warm beneath the chamois skin with her brother on one side and her grandmother on the other. She did not speak because she wanted to think before the others started moving about. She remembered the first time she had ever shot an arrow. Old Tsona had been teaching Gishay and she had stood watching and listening.

"You hold it straight with the eye like this," old Tsona had said, pointing the bow at a young baobab tree.

Gishay was a difficult student. He preferred playing guessing games or tumbling on a sand dune with the other boys his age. He missed the baobab with the arrow three times over.

Khuana, who had come trailing behind her old grand-

16

mother with a load of wood on her head, had seen them. She dropped the wood and ran to old Tsona, then waited patiently until Gishay had sent two more arrows in the direction of the baobab.

Old Tsona ignored Khuana and said to Gaushe: "I chose this baobab because it has a thick trunk, but this boy can only run, play, and imitate other people. What can I do with him?"

Gaushe smiled, but Khuana said: "I can listen, our old Tsona. Teach me, please! Please!"

Tsona, who was about to send her away with words about men's work and her sticking to carrying firewood and grub hunting, saw the earnest look in Khuana's eyes and realized this was his chance to teach the inattentive Gishay a lesson. Even now Gishay looked over his shoulder, hoping for the right moment to escape, to run and play with the other boys.

"Please! Please! Our old Tsona," Khuana begged.

Because she always watched everything the hunters did so intensely, Tsona had given her the name Little-Sharp-Eye. Now he said, "Why do you want to shoot, Little-Sharp-Eye?"

"I want to shoot the gemsbok and the springbok."

"You won't be allowed to go with the hunters," old Tsona reminded her.

"But if a gemsbok wanders into our camp like that one did during the last rains and there were only women there, I could shoot it."

Out of the corner of his eye old Tsona could see Gishay glancing about for his playmates.

"Go on, Gishay," old Tsona said a little peevishly. "Go on, you don't want to learn. I'll teach Khuana to shoot."

17

Khuana jumped up and down, the beads dancing in her hair.

"Thank you, old Tsona, our old Tsona!"

"Arrows are dangerous," old Tsona had begun. "Never point them at anyone. They have poison on them." He taught her how to hold the bow and fit it with an arrow.

Khuana had never tried to shoot before. She had touched and rubbed the smooth wood of her father's bow and had once hefted his arrow, but she had never tried to shoot. Now in her excitement she completely missed the baobab bush three times, but after that she hit it twice and missed once. Old Tsona praised her as an apt pupil and said he wished Gishay would do as well.

Khuana lay quietly beside her grandmother and brother and thought about her first lesson from old Tsona.

Usually the men were up by this time. They were not up this morning because Cripple Guike's report of sighting a great chamois three nights' sleeps away had kept them busy planning and dancing and asking Gao Na for success in the hunt until late in the night. Khuana had also prayed to Gao Na, asking him to let her find an ostrich and to bless her arrows in the hunt. Khuana had arrows hidden away in a small bag that she carried beneath her kaross. She had planned it all well and nothing could go wrong.

At this moment, Khuana turned her head and was momentarily blinded by strong light, and looking out across the open desert, she saw the morning sun strike the desert like a hammer hitting an anvil and send splashing sparks of gold across the sand.

Khuana smiled as she wiggled her toes in the sand. The morning was chilly and she retreated under the chamois

18

skin. Soon it would be warm enough to get up. In the distance she heard the desert grouse call. She stretched herself and smiled, pleased with life.

Throughout the camp others heard the grouse call, and suddenly, the magic stillness fled from the morning. Men and women yawned, stretched, and uncoiled themselves from the cocoonlike hides in which they slept. The werf came alive. "Morro!" was chanted across from skerm to skerm as people laughed and greeted each other as if they were happy that Gao Na had let them pass another night. Old Tsona began to stir the embers of the fire as people moved in closer to it. Khuana's mother got up and tucked the chamois skin closer around her brother and, in a low-pitched conversation with her grandmother, started making plans for breakfast and the day's food gathering.

Her father joined the hunters, and the five men, casting long shadows to the west, set off across the sand. They had not eaten breakfast and Khuana knew they would search for food on the way.

3

The Search

They ran in the direction of the sun. Khuana saw their figures, like dark stick-men on the surface of the sand, move behind a sand dune and disappear as though they had vanished into the sun.

Nsue rushed up and greeted her: "Good sun!"

"Good sun to you."

Nsue was one girl who didn't need ostrich-shell beads in her hair to make her beautiful, Khuana thought. Her skin was as smooth and as brown as a gourd. She always seemed to smile no matter what her worries. She smiled now.

"Where will you and your old grandmother search for food today?" she asked Khuana.

"First we'll follow that omuramba for part of a shadow. Then we'll turn upon the land to try to find those tsama melons."

The fire was dying out as the sun rose higher. Mothers were suckling their babies. Soon they would leave them in the care of small children or old grandmothers who could no longer hunt for food. Children chased each other in front of the skerms and slid down small sand dunes; their laughter rang like music in the silent desert.

Khuana did not mention the other part of their plan, which was to find a marula tree and to search for the little white pupae.

"Where will you and your mother collect today?"

"We'll search for roots, grubs, and dried onions. The tops of the onion leaves are dry and may have been blown off by the winds but we shall try to find them with digging sticks."

"Khuana, you know it's a good thing Guike sighted that chamois yesterday or things would be different."

"Yes, it's a good thing," Khuana agreed. "But what do you mean different?"

"Well, I heard old Tsona and your father Kwi talking just before Guike came back and he said that the water is foul and will be completely gone in three days. Old Tsona said it is best to move on while we have enough water to last us until we reach the next water hole."

"It's true about the water. It makes me sick to drink it. So I suppose if we get meat, we can stay longer. I hope they bring back the chamois."

"I do, too. The meat is good, but I sometimes hate to drink the water from the antelope's stomach."

"Khuana, Khuana, let's go!" her grandmother called.

"Bring me a special little root, Nsue. Please! I want something from you."

"And you bring me the dried leaves of the infata bush for sweet women's scents."

Khuana ran past skerms to a place on the edge of the camp where her old grandmother waited for her. She was surprised to find the camp almost empty. She and her grandmother searched for roots along the shallow banks of the omuramba. In places sand had drifted into the river, filling the river valley and bringing it to the level of the surrounding land. When the rains come, she thought, this river bank will bloom with good food plants. Once Khuana thought she saw a small animal move, but when she rushed to it, she found only a small round hole with the sand being sucked in with continuous breathlike whiffs. The sand rolled in a kind of circle. She worked on it with her digging stick, but the faster she dug, the more sand came in to fill it up.

"What did you see?" Gaushe stood watching.

"A desert mouse, I think," replied Khuana.

"Anyway, it's gone now. There are not many animals left here. There is not much of anything, now. The men say we should move on to Guatscha pan. If we don't move the men think we'll be trapped here during the worst part of the dry season with not enough water to get us there."

Khuana knew that there was usually enough water at Guatscha pan. But there would be many bands of Bushmen there, and to make the water last over the whole dry season, bands stayed in their regular camping areas until all food and water were used up. The Bushmen only went to the Guatscha pan when they were driven there by hunger and thirst. It would be good to see Dikai again. She would also be ten travels old now, like Nsue and herself. Then there was her Aunt Dolia who had married into another camp, and many cousins whom Khuana loved.

"When will we leave?" Khuana asked.

"Last night, they said in two sleeps. Now it depends on that chamois. If they kill it, we can eat here a week then suck enough water from the earth to go on."

"And if there is no chamois?" Khuana said.

"Then we leave in another day's time, I think."

They walked up the omuramba, the grandmother in front setting a brisk pace. She had always been a hard worker and a shrewd collector of food. Whenever anyone was hungry in the camp, they were sure to find an extra root, seed, or melon in her grandmother's bag. She could trace a melon even if the dried vine was buried in the sand.

"You are still fast on your feet, grandmother."

The grandmother looked back at Khuana and smiled. "The little one is tired?"

"No," Khuana said truthfully.

She had been pushed backward by the unstable, sinking sand, but she enjoyed its trickle through her toes. Now the sand was cool—later when the sun moved higher, it would burn the flesh. With the exception of a few parched bushes growing beside the stream bed, the desert landscape looked the same in all directions.

There was no landmark to tell where to go. Yet, Gaushe knew. After a while she said, "We turn here."

"Your eyes are still keen," said Khuana.

"The old are fast and useful or they're left behind," Gaushe answered.

Whenever anyone spoke of leaving an old person be-

24

hind, Khuana's eyes became serious, her fist clenched at her side, and her small, smooth jaw set firmly. Khuana felt unhappy because she loved the old people of her band, especially her grandmother. She had never known anyone to be left behind since she was born, but there were stories saying that when all hope was lost it could happen.

"We'll never leave you behind, grandmother."

Gaushe smiled at her seriousness. "Don't be so serious. It was just a joke, little rebel."

Khuana did not think of herself as a rebel. She only opposed those things that to her seemed wrong. She could run as fast as any boy her age and had beaten many of them when they wrestled together until she was ten years old and her mother made her stop wrestling. Old Tsona himself had said Khuana was a natural marksman and she could track as quietly as anyone. So far, everyone believed her brother had shot the guinea fowl he brought into the camp during the last wet season. In fact, Khuana had shot the bird. Everyone gave her brother the praise which was rightfully hers, saying he would someday be a fine hunter. She didn't envy him the praise; he needed it after being blamed for playing about so much. But it showed how unjust was the taboo against women and girls hunting. Khuana could hunt almost as well as a man.

After they left the omuramba, old Gaushe's pace quickened. She scanned the horizon, shading her eyes with her wrinkled hand. After a moment, she pointed at a low sand dune and into a grove of thorn trees, shrubs, and parched grasses.

"There it is! There it is!" Khuana shouted, running toward the marula tree. She pulled off bits of its bark searching for cocoons.

"Not there," Gaushe said. "Take your stick. Dig in the ground around the trunk like this."

Khuana dug fast and intently with her digging stick, the sand flying away and striking her kaross. "Nothing. I see nothing," Khuana said.

But Gaushe had moved to another side of the tree. "The sun is over your shoulder," she said. "You won't find any there or on the opposite side of the tree. Beetles choose the side where there is less drying. Let's try here." She made a few light strokes in the sand. Below the surface the sand was moist. "You see, there's a little moisture."

Near the trunk of the tree, they uncovered them. In the gray, damp sand five cocoons lay like pieces of green jade. The shells were moist but would dry to brittleness.

Khuana held one in her hand and jumped for joy in the sand. "Here's my ostrich egg! Here's my ostrich egg! You're going to get an ostrich egg canteen for me," she said to the pupa.

She suddenly stopped dancing, rebuking herself. Was she an ungrateful and discourteous child? She had not thanked her grandmother. She hugged her grandmother tightly and kissed her a hundred times.

"Thank you dear grandmother, our old grandmother. Fortune was mine when Gao Na gave you to me."

Old Gaushe's eyes misted as she struck out half-heartedly at a fly. When she spoke, her voice was gentle.

"Silly, wonderful child. You make me break our laws and say Gao Na sent me to help you disobey." She shook her head and the two moved off, the child's head buried under the circle of the arm of the grandmother. The sun behind them cast a single shadow on the harsh Kalahari desert.

"Let's hurry. We've collected no food and the sun is high."

They hunted for roots, berries, and melons until noon, but they found very little. Then as they went back along the omuramba, Gaushe remembered a place where she had seen three tsama melons growing during the last rains. They went back up the omuramba and took one of its many turnings, searching all around the remembered spot. But there was nothing. The high sand dunes and crumpled, dry desert grasses yielded nothing. The sun, now very high and hot, made Khuana and her grandmother pant and move along very slowly. Finally they scrambled up the side of the riverbed, having sighted the camp. As they approached the camp, Khuana cried, "Oh! I forgot them."

"The pupae are in your bag," her grandmother said.

"I mean the scented leaves for Nsue."

Old Gaushe reached into her kaross. "I know how you like them and since there was no food to fill my kaross, I picked some back in the omuramba." As she handed the dried brown leaves to Khuana, the leaves gave off an odor like a mixture of jasmine and cinnamon.

4

Games in the Sand

Many women and children had returned to their skerms earlier and now lay quietly in the shade in shallow holes covered with branches. Some slept; almost no one talked. That was unusual, thought Khuana, but she was too tired to think very long about it. Khuana and her grandmother stumbled into a skerm to rest. Before long Khuana too was sleeping. She awoke very hungry and thirsty.

Khuana took a small pot and ran down to the water hole. She didn't see the women peep out at her from the shelter of their skerms and shake their heads with sadness. On her way to the water hole, she missed the foul odor of the water. The smell usually met her long before she reached the place. This time she smelled nothing. Then, standing on the edge of the depression in the sand, she looked down into the water hole. She felt sick and nauseated. She flopped down weakly in the sand. Now she knew why everyone in the camp was sad. They didn't tell you when something was wrong because nobody liked to carry bad news. As the saying went, the bearer of bad news is the cause of the bad news. He not only brought bad news but kept away good news. Cripple Guike had a story about it, a story he called the good news bird and the bad news bird. And he told how painful it was for each of these birds to learn to fly. That's why they never came at the same time.

The water was all gone. Where the foul-smelling, but life-giving water had been, the earth was dry and veined with spidery fissures running along the bottom of the hole. Khuana looked at the hole and back at the cooking pot. She had never thought she could miss that foul-smelling water! Now, she knew how important even that was to their survival. She picked up her pot and went back to the camp toward the skerm where the women sat cooking. She sat down near one of the skerms; Khuana's mother saw her and brought a pot over for her to clean.

"It was a shock to me," said Khuana's mother without looking at her. "I was surprised when the men said last night we might go so soon."

She and old Gaushe watched Khuana as she scoured the pot with grass and sand, and both grandmother and mother were proud of their daughter. She never complained of thirst. She simply kept busy and did her work with a lively spirit. They knew she would never be easily defeated. They were also proud she was growing into such a beautiful girl with useful limbs.

Khuana knew the many difficulties the Bushmen had to face as the dry season went on. Now there were no game animals, no roots, and no rodents. There was the heat of the sun, no water, and the horrible pain of daily hunger. But Khuana was not frightened that they would die. She knew they would find water. She was not frightened of moving because the men of the camp knew where to go. They were not just wandering aimlessly; they had a set goal: an oasis ten sleeps away, where there was plenty of water, ample food, friends, and members of one's family. It would be good to greet these people again after an absence of three rainy seasons. Cousins would have grown bigger, aunts were older and probably had other children. Then there was the news of the old—and the dead; things of sadness that your eyes only told you because of the absence of a remembered, gay, wrinkled face with smiling eyes; or of hands that once swiftly and skillfully made ostrich-shell beads for your hair or shot an antelope for your kaross. These were things to be met at the end of the journey. So why not begin; fight the desert if it fights you; live with it in all its moods.

But there was another reason why Khuana was happy to travel. Her reason had nothing to do with oases, relatives, or campfires. She turned this over in her mind as she scooped a handful of sand into the cooking pot and gave it a thorough scouring, her hands moving the ball of dried grass roughly over the inner surface of the pot. She thought to herself: it may be my chance to get an ostrich. The ostriches have moved near to water. If they find plenty they can lay eggs at any time but if there's no water they won't nest until the rains come so that the chicks will have plenty to eat. If we are on the move we may find some, but there's none about here. She looked in the direction of the dry water hole.

"Khuana, Khuana," her mother called, "please bring me that pot as the hare would." Khuana knew this meant quickly. She ran, carrying it to her mother.

30

Her mother took the pot and started putting in desert onions.

"Take off your kaross and help with the baby."

"Oh mother, may I keep it on? I've got Nsue's scented leaves in it."

"Yes, here, take the baby for a while."

Khuana took the fat baby in her arms and walked down the sand between the skerms. Here and there the camp children played. Khuana passed by a group of boys sitting in two lines facing each other and playing their guessing game. Gishay sat on the edge of the crowd, watching. She held up the baby. He laughed and Khuana moved on until she came to the skerms of Nsue's family. In the sand nearby some girls of six and seven years were building a skerm.

She spotted Nsue helping her mother peel wild onions for soup and she raised her hand high in greeting, "Morro, Nsue."

"Morro," Nsue called back. "I'll be finished in a little while."

She turned to Ungka, Nsue's six-year-old sister, an absentminded girl who usually played by herself and soon forgot anything she was told.

"Here, you mind the baby for me, please."

Nsue still smelled of onions, but Khuana grabbed her hands. "I've got them. I've got your scented leaves, but I don't know if you can smell them after peeling onions." Khuana removed her kaross from her shoulders, took out the scented leaves, and laid the kaross beside her on the sand.

"Oh, it doesn't matter whether I smell them today or not. They say we are to set out tomorrow for Guatscha

31

pan where there's plenty of water and food. There will be lots of relatives, friends, feasts and dancing. Oh Khuana, think of it, we will have lots of time to comb our hair, plait beads, and wear sweet scents."

Khuana smiled at the happiness on the face of her friend.

"Oh, thank you Khuana, for my scented leaves, but I'm sorry I could find nothing you liked. There's nothing here." She waved her hand over the desert. "No food. We searched all morning and found only one or two wild onions."

"Don't worry Nsue, if grandmother hadn't helped me I would not have brought you the leaves. But how do you know we are leaving tomorrow? Grandmother said we'd go only if the men returned without meat."

"Khuana, the hunters have returned, and some of the women overheard old Tsona talking when they failed to bring back meat. 'The animals are gone,' he said. 'The water hole is dry, the tsama melons are bitter,' Tsona said. 'We must also go after one sleep!' "

"I am glad it's true. Now I can make plans in case we meet ostriches on the way. Look, let me show you . . ." She reached down for her kaross but it was not there. Her fingers touched sand. "It was here only a moment ago." She got up quickly and scanned the sand.

"Oh, I bet my sister Ungka took it," Nsue said.

Khuana looked about for Ungka, but she was not in sight. She forgot about the kaross when she found the baby was also missing. Her pulse came quicker. She bit her lip. Where could the baby be? Perhaps he had just toddled into one of the skerms. Khuana and Nsue started a search.

"Have you seen Ungka? Where did Ungka go?" they asked the girls who still played beside their tiny skerms, but no one knew where Ungka had disappeared to with the baby.

Khuana and Nsue stood up and called "Ungka!" but there was no answer.

The camp was in a thicket of dried brown bushes with skerms built in a circle. Beyond this was the dry riverbed and nothing but sand dunes and sand on the other side, as far as the eye could see. Where could a child and baby disappear to in the camp and how far could they go in such a short time? There was no point in looking for tracks, for there were so many footprints leading in and out of the camp that it would be impossible to distinguish Ungka's tracks. Still, Khuana knew she must find the baby before her mother came to feed him.

"Nsue, you go that way toward our skerm and I'll take this side of the camp. We'll meet back here." They both ran off looking into skerms as they went and calling, "Ungka! Ungka!"

Khuana must have looked in every skerm and under every chamois or gemsbok blanket in her end of the camp. By the time they met again in front of Nsue's skerm, Nsue had done the same. But neither of them had seen any sign of Ungka and the baby. Khuana was now fully alarmed. Her heart beat so fast she thought it would burst, and she wrung her hands thinking of how upset her mother would be.

"Oh, what can we do, Nsue? Where can they be?"

Nsue looked around herself. There were tears in her eyes. Through her blurred vision, she saw to one side of the camp the riverbed with its water hole now dry, and to the other side the high sand dune that sheltered the camp from the fierce evening sun. "There are only two places left, now." Khuana's eyes followed Nsue's as she spoke. "They're either in the water hole or on the other side of that sand dune."

"Come on, then. You look at the water hole, I'll look behind the sand dune," Khuana said.

But Nsue caught her hand. "I'll come with you. If they'd gone to the water hole someone in the camp would have seen them."

The two girls stopped short, however, at the sound of Khuana's mother calling.

"Khuana, Khuana, bring the baby. I want to feed him."

"Oh Nsue, I hope they are there," she said, as they ran to the sand dune.

They ran around the rippling sand waves of the dune and there they saw a welcome sight: Ungka, holding the baby on her lap in front of her, was giving the baby a fine time. It laughed and gurgled as Ungka slid down the sand, picked herself up off the ground again with difficulty, and, carrying her load, walked stumblingly back up the side of the dune and slid down again. They both laughed and waved as Khuana and Nsue came up to them.

"Oh, Ungka," said Khuana, "why didn't you answer me?"

"I didn't hear," said Ungka, as she started up the sand dune again, but Nsue caught the baby from her. Khuana picked up her kaross, which had fallen in the sand.

"Ungka, you naughty one. Let me see if my precious things are here." She opened the kaross, found the two arrowheads, and began looking for cocoons. There were only four. "Two of my poison cocoons are missing."

"What's this?" cried Nsue, pointing to the baby's hand which held something to its moist lips.

"Oh, look," said Khuana, "the baby is trying to eat that cocoon." The two girls stared at each other, horrified. Khuana took the cocoon away and dropped it in the kaross. "It's a good thing he couldn't open the cocoon."

"Khuana! Khuana, bring the baby!" her mother called. She dropped the kaross and grabbed the baby.

"Wait here, I'll be back, Nsue," she said.

After she'd given her baby brother to her mother and returned to the sand dune, she and Nsue searched all around the sand but couldn't find the lost cocoon.

"Did you search, Ungka?"

"Yes, Ungka didn't have it. It's probably buried in the sand."

"Khuana, don't tell me this is more to do with your silly idea of hunting? Are you going to poison arrows?"

"Yes, Nsue."

"But Khuana, something terrible may happen. Just look at what almost happened to the baby."

"That's the last time I'll let them out of my sight. I'll be more careful next time."

"Still, I'm frightened," said Nsue.

Nsue observed the seriousness of Khuana's face, and

by her flashing dark eyes, she knew Khuana's mind was made up, and she wouldn't change it.

"Since you won't change your mind, I'll say no more against it," Nsue said. They were silent for a moment; then she went on: "Ostrich eggshell canteens are beautiful. Did you see the one my aunt had when we met them last dry season?" said Nsue. "That was such a big egg it could hold enough water for two people for three days."

The two friends walked slowly back to the camp.

"And the decorations! Remember the lovely red and black patterns on the polished, creamy white of the ostrich eggshell?" said Khuana.

"And there was a plug to close the smooth hole. I think it was made of soft wood."

"A circle of beads that ended in a holder for the ostrich eggshell canteen was strung around your aunt's neck. I want one like that, Nsue, and I know I can shoot an ostrich myself."

"Why don't you just find the ostrich away from its nest and take an egg or two?" said Nsue.

"It's not so hard; let me show you how it's done." Khuana pulled out of her kaross two pointed arrowheads. "These were some imperfect ones that father was throwing away." She also brought out two strong, hollow reeds.

"Do you also have a bow in your kaross?" Nsue laughed in amazement.

"No, but grandma will let me have the one grandpa left her when he died. Look Nsue, this hollow reed fits over the blunt end of the arrow. The poison goes right here on the shaft behind the tip. I saw the men do it last night. Now when that strikes an animal he can brush against a tree and lose the reed, but the arrow stays until the animal falls down because of the poison."

Nsue looked around to see if anyone had overheard Khuana's proposal for breaking the law of the tribe.

"You mean you'll put the poison on the arrows by yourself?"

"If my grandmother watches for me. But Nsue, you are my best friend and the only other person I've told. Come with me."

"No, Khuana, I am afraid. It will get us into trouble."

"The only thing it will get us are canteens. Come on, Nsue. There's an old moon tonight. Meet me upriver past the water hole. There will be a small fire. Please, Nsue."

"I'll try, Khuana, but don't see evil if I don't come."

5

The Accident

The rising moon shone like sparkling diamonds on the desert sand. Here and there in the clear, quiet sky, stars fluttered and twinkled like broken pieces of white shell in blue sand. The night was cool and though there was a bright fire in the center of the camp, there was little laughter. The men had returned without meat. There had been a dust storm in that part of the desert and the tracks had disappeared. They had searched all morning, and finding nothing, returned, thinking Cripple Guike's chamois a mirage or ghost of some past killed chamois come back to haunt the Bushman band. Now the men sat alone, thinking and planning. The women sat around the fire, joking, gossiping, and laughing at the play of their children. Even with them, the laughter was not as loud as usual. After throwing a look at Nsue, Khuana left the fire to join her grandmother, who had already made a small fire behind the steep bank of the omuramba.

Gaushe did not ask Khuana any questions, and Khuana was glad, for her grandmother had pleaded with her to give up her hunting. Gaushe wrapped the chamois skin robe closer around her shoulders and Khuana sat with her knees drawn up toward her chin, her arms folded around them. She stared into the fire and said:

"Old Tsona can see things in the fire when he dances the moon dance. He can tell if the journey will be good, if the antelope will be plentiful, or how soon to expect the rains. Can you see things in the fire, grandmother? Will I kill a chamois or an ostrich?"

"I'm afraid I haven't got Tsona's power to see, my daughter. His father, old Samgau, was even better at it than Tsona. He used to tell who would shoot the animal during a hunt."

"Do you think we will see ostriches on our journey to Guatscha pan, grandmother?"

"That's not easy to say, my daughter. There are two ways to Guatscha pan; one is straight across the desert for ten sleeps, the other is down this omuramba, across the desert, and around the hills. That takes about six sleeps but it is considered more dangerous."

"How could it be more dangerous if it's shorter?"

"All our bands used to cross that way. Then seven rains ago we had a long dry season and tried to make Guatscha pan by the low hills. In the sandy valley we found all the water holes dry. Guatscha pan was still four sleeps away, and without water ten of our number died."

A tear gleamed in old Gaushe's eyes. "That was the season we lost your grandfather. He refused his share of the little water that remained and nine others were left with him. We left him on the second day. He was already dead—dried out. We built him and two others a skerm in the hot sand and left them. I wouldn't leave him but the others picked me up and carried me away. My eyes and chest almost burst within me." She quickly wiped her eyes. "They promised to send young men back with water when we reached the pan. But as we were all exhausted, it took us five sleeps to get to the pan and another four for the young men to come back. I never had any hope for him as I had seen him dead before I left him, but I wanted to die too. They wouldn't let me. When the young men found them after nine days they were completely dried out." Another tear shone on Gaushe's wrinkled skin.

Khuana moved near and put her arms around Gaushe. "Poor, dear grandmother. How terrible for you."

Gaushe kept talking as if the sound of her voice was necessary to comfort her. "There used to be plenty of green plants and good water holes around those hills even during a dry season, and there were lots of animals in that valley—even ostriches. But since that dry season seven years ago, old Tsona won't go near the valley. He says it was an act of Gao Na. Samgau himself had foreseen it and had told Tsona about it years before, but Tsona ignored him and he still feels responsible for those who died. So we go straight across the desert. There are only two water holes between here and the pan but these two holes always give enough water to last."

"Anyway, I'll be prepared if we see an ostrich." Khuana laid out her cocoons, ready to poison her arrowheads. She looked all around. "Nsue isn't coming," she said. "I think she's afraid."

41

Khuana opened the cocoon as she had seen her father do. She prized open the brittle structure with the tip of her arrow, holding the reed near the arrow shaft. She did it very clumsily, dropping the cocoon three times before she had opened it. "This arrow should be sharpened," she said to Gaushe, who looked on, amused. Now she used the arrows, scraping the remaining pieces of brittle covering the silvery body, and there the pupa was alive, wriggling slightly. As she was about to put the poison on the arrow, Khuana said, "Poor, frightened Nsue. She doesn't know what fun she's going to miss." Khuana looked up at her grandmother to see the old woman watching her closely with something like disapproval in her eyes. Khuana hesitated. "What is it, grandmother?"

Gaushe looked at her more closely, as a teacher might regard hopefully a failing student. "Did you say you watched the men closely when they did this?" Gaushe asked.

"I did, grandmother, first they looked . . ." Then she remembered: "Oh . . . oh." She threw down the pupa and arrow as though they were crawling desert lizards.

"First they looked at their hands to see there were no broken places through which the poison could enter. How could I have forgotten that?"

Khuana dared not meet her grandmother's eyes. She looked sheepishly at her fingers, even looking under the ends of her fingernails. She could have cut herself with a digging stick. Then she picked up her things again and smeared the poison on the arrow, crushing the beetle pupa, rubbing its juice behind the arrowhead.

Old Gaushe, adjusting her chamois shawl against the cooling night and stretching her wrinkled legs toward the fire, watched silently. Small pieces of dried grass and grains of sand stuck to her legs where they had lain in the sand. When Khuana finished an arrow, Gaushe held it over the fire to dry.

While she was drying an arrow and Khuana was opening a third cocoon, the accident happened. It had been an unusually hard cocoon to open but Khuana kept at it. Despite her efforts to prevent it, the arrow slipped into the body of the white pupa, showing the split flesh through the brittle shell. Khuana was a bit disgusted. She took that arrow from its reed shaft, put it aside, and took a fresh arrow. Then, biting her bottom lip, she gave the covering several fast slashes with the arrowhead, with all her might. Suddenly, the arrowhead slipped off the brittle cover of the pupa with so much force that Khuana could no longer control its movement. The poisoned arrowhead struck old Gaushe's leg, making a deep stab wound in her leg.

Khuana dropped the arrow as though it was red hot and fell down on her knees. Shaking all over with fear, she grabbed and held her grandmother's leg. Her heart beat as if to break open her breast and tears fell from her eyes. "Oh, what have I done? What have I done?" The tears came fast and hot, falling on old Gaushe's leg.

"Does it hurt, grandmother? I am so sorry, grandmother." The words poured out of Khuana. "I'll clean it. Let me! Oh, I must suck the poison out!"

Gaushe, because she was older and more experienced, did not think of the wound first. She did not feel any pain as the arrow went into her skin. Some time passed before she felt needlelike pains shooting up her leg. Even then, she did not cry out. There was only a slight change

—a widening of the eyes. But Khuana saw this and was even more alarmed. Her heart pounded in her breast as she hastily bent down to her grandmother's leg, and held it.

Gaushe said, "I don't think there was any poison, but we must make sure. If you are going to suck it out, you must not forget and swallow it. You know what will happen if you do."

Alarm grew on Khuana's face—alarm for her grandmother's safety. Her eyes widened and she was near to panic. She felt terrible. "Oh, I've killed you, grandmother. I've killed you because of my selfishness."

She threw herself on Gaushe's leg, crying. Sobs shook her body.

"I don't care what happens to me," she said earnestly, "the poison must come out."

With the feel of warm tears on her face, Khuana took a small sharp piece of stone from her kaross and cut an X-shaped gash in her grandmother's skin, over the wound. Then, bending with her mouth to the wound, she sucked the place and spat into the sand. She cried silently all the while and fear was a cold lump in her chest. She sucked and spat, and sucked again. The poison must come out! It must come out! Finally her grandmother stopped her.

"Now, now, my child."

Cold sweat ran down Khuana's back and she lay with her head on her old grandmother, holding the injured leg as if to let it go would be to see her sink away beneath the sea of sand and be lost forever.

Finally she spoke. "Will it . . . will it be all right, grandmother?"

Gaushe tried to be cheerful. "With a doctor as good as old Tsona, I think so."

"Has this ever happened to anyone . . . who lived on?"

"Not exactly this way."

"I couldn't bear to lose you, grandmother." She got up. "I am going to call old Tsona to make sure the poison is completely out of your leg."

She started away, but her grandmother called her in a firm voice. "No Khuana, I'm sure you got all of the poison out. All I fear now is the swelling and soreness."

"Perhaps it won't swell and will be all right tomorrow," Khuana said hopefully. They sat silent for a long while. Khuana hoped everyone would be sleeping when they walked back into camp. She was glad now Nsue had not come. Nsue would hate her. Everyone would hate her now.

In the cool of the next morning old Gaushe awoke and immediately discovered she could not move her leg. People began rolling up their chamois blankets, filling their karosses with their possessions, and tearing down skerms ready for the journey to Guatscha pan. But old Gaushe couldn't move the leg. Khuana, who had slept by her side, realized something was wrong and woke with a fright. "How is it, old grandmother?" she said, wiping the sleep from her eyes.

"Not good, child. I can't move it."

Khuana, near to tears, again began rubbing the leg. "Maybe it went to sleep during the night," she said hopefully. "What do you feel? Something like thorns?"

"No, only a drumlike pain. It feels like a piece of rotted wood."

Khuana was quite afraid now. Ever since the accident

46

she had been gripped with fear—fear growing upon her, weighing her down. She looked at her grandmother and wanted to scream. She loved her so.

The fear had grown all through the night. She didn't know at first why this cold, gloomy feeling followed her everywhere. It almost crushed her during her sleep. But by morning it was clear to her what it was and why it seemed real, a thing she could almost touch. It had begun last night when they came back to find everyone gathered around the fire in the center of the camp.

When she and her grandmother returned and were seated with the rest in front of the crackling fire, an anxious silence fell over the place. Old Tsona began speaking.

"Our Gao Na has seen fit to keep us in health and food at this pan for many sleeps. Now as the sun's hammer strikes the anvil harder and rays fly over the entire desert the heat burns away life. The plants dry up; the desert drinks our water, and the animals vanish toward an unknown forest. It is time we moved from the sun's fierce stare." He paused, and looked around him at the other men, and continued: "We men have talked together. We leave tomorrow before the sun's hammer beats away the chill. Our Kwi shall get us enough water to take us over nine sleeps of desert. We travel until the first water drops from our faces, then we dig holes and sleep until night quiets the desert's anger. Then we go on. It will be a hard journey. We would have gone a week ago if we had known the water in our pan would leave us so unexpectedly."

Everyone was silent. When old Tsona spoke, that was the end of the matter.

Nsue ran over to greet Khuana when the meeting was finished, caught her hand and said:

"You're not angry I didn't come, are you?"

"Why didn't you?"

"I was scared. You know all the rules against women using hunting tools. Give it up, Khuana. We can have just as much fun finding scented leaves, plaiting ostrich-shell beads in our hair, and decorating karosses."

Khuana did not answer. She only looked thoughtful. She knew now her friend spoke the truth. But quickly she told herself it had been an accident and would not have happened if she had been properly trained as the boys were.

"Please Khuana," Nsue pressed her hand. "I am afraid. Something is bound to happen!"

Something had already "happened" and Khuana, too, was afraid. Now, she knew exactly what the fear was. She had never seen an old person left behind in her life-time. She had been very lucky. All of the people she knew had died in camp among their families and friends. But she had overheard some of the adults refer to some old person who had been left behind because they could no longer keep up. She had thought it terribly cruel to leave an old person to face the desert and desert jackals alone. But the children, even Nsue, had said that at times like those the leader had to think of everybody. Was it right to endanger the lives of all young members of the camp to save the life of an old person who might not live a year? Someone who was already dead, so to speak?

Now, rubbing old Gaushe's leg, she knew that it was

this fear that caused her heart to beat faster, her breath to come in short gasps. It was this unwelcome thought that caused her to shiver in the early morning chill.

The leg grew warmer as she rubbed it. She could not tell if it was from the warmth of her own fingers or if it was heat from her grandmother's body. Old Gaushe sat impassively, looking at all the people folding their chamois skins, tying their cooking pots into bundles, and hurrying here and there through the sand.

"Khuana," her mother called from nearby. But Khuana did not answer. She was folding the chamois blanket closely around Gaushe's body. She looked at Gaushe's leg and her eyes widened. A smile broke on her flat face. She threw herself upon her grandmother's neck, kissing her sweet, old, wrinkled face. Gaushe was nearly knocked backward in the sand.

"What is it? What is it my child?" she said, gasping for breath.

"Your toes, your toes. You're moving them."

Gaushe looked at her feet and tears streamed down her face. "Yes, they're moving."

"Can you bend your knee, grandmother?"

"Khuana!" her mother called impatiently.

"Yes, mother, coming."

But she was in no hurry to leave old Gaushe, who was trying to move her knee but found it painful. It bent only a little.

"Khuana! You must come and help with the baby, *now*," her mother said with finality.

"Keep trying, grandmother, I'll be right back!" She raced off. When in a few minutes Khuana came back carrying her fat baby brother, Gaushe was up and walking with only a slight limp. Khuana was overcome with happiness.

"See grandmother walk," she said to the baby. "She's walking, walking," she said tossing the baby into the air and catching him.

"Khuana don't do that!" Her mother came by carrying a rolled grass mat and a chamois skin. "You may drop the baby." Then, she noticed her mother's limp. "Mother, what's wrong with you?"

With that question, Khuana stopped still, expecting the whole camp to come running and her old grandmother to say, "Khuana stabbed me with a poisoned arrow." Then there would be her mother's scream and general alarm and sorrow in the camp. But even as she thought about it, Gaushe answered quietly without giving the whole truth: "The night was very cold and today I'm stiff."

Khuana's heart went out to her old grandmother who would not betray her. "If they ever leave you, dear old grandmother," she whispered in her heart, "they shall also leave Khuana."

"Well," said Khuana's mother moving on with her work, "no doubt the coming sun," she nodded towards the egg-yellow spatter on the sandy eastern horizon, "will soon scorch away your stiffness. Hurry and roll up your things, mother; already my husband, Kwi, is beginning to draw water for our journey and soon we shall be gone to Guatscha pan."

6

March on the Desert

When her mother had gone, Khuana and her grand-mother looked at each other. They were very happy.

"I know I can get through the first day," her grand-mother finally said, "for they will not march long before the sun comes up. If it was a wet season or if we were in the valleys around those hills, I'd soon be well because I'd find healing leaves to bathe the wound."

"Anyway," Khuana said, thoughtfully, "we'll get to Guatscha pan."

While her grandmother rolled the chamois skin into a bundle for carrying, Khuana saw Nsue rushing by on the other side of the camp. Nsue saw her at the same time and shouted, "Morro! Come on! Don't you want to see your father draw water from a dried-up water hole? Everybody is looking."

They went down to the omuramba and stood around the dried water hole where her father and old Tsona looked at the dried, cracked soil. Gishay stood nearby with a water skin.

"Oh," said Nsue with disappointment. "I am sure we won't get to Guatscha pan now. No one can get water where there's none."

"Just because you don't see it, it doesn't mean it isn't there," said old Mrs. Samgau. "You haven't seen Gao Na, yet you believe in him."

"But it's dry," said Khuana. "Even drier than when I tried to dig up water."

"Still, there's water. There's water there, I'm certain," old Mrs. Samgau said.

Kwi removed a square of the hard-caked earth and tossed it aside. The soil of the spot, a mixture of dirt and sand, showed a dark stain which Khuana knew to be dampness. But still there was no water in sight.

Khuana's father dug away more and more of the soil from the hole until his hands were sticky with mud. Then he took two hollow reeds, put bits of grass in one end, and bending on his knees, pushed the reeds deep into the mud. He covered the end of the reeds with his mouth and sucked. His jaws on either side moved inward until he looked as if he had no teeth. The muscles in his jaws quivered. The veins stood out like twisted brown vines on his forehead, and though he was naked to the waist and the chill of the morning had not yet been burnt away, little rivulets of sweat coursed down his face and head. The rivulets of sweat flowed into the hollow at the back of his neck and coursed around each side meeting underneath his chin, finally dropping onto the mud just near the place where the reed entered the earth.

Kwi never stopped to take a full breath, and just as it

52

seemed he would fall on his face from exhaustion, his slackened, sunken jaws began to bulge outward. His jaws ballooned as though they were filling with air. Khuana's face cracked in a wide smile when her father left the reeds sticking in the sand and raised his head; water flowed from the reeds and from the corners of his mouth.

"You see," said old Samgau's wife looking around triumphantly, as though she had done it herself. Old Tsona now said there was more water here than they had expected and that everyone should have a drink, fill their water skins, and be ready to move off toward Guatscha pan.

When the band of thirty-one men, women, and children set out across the desert, Khuana carried her share of the family belongings, which was a rolled skin containing her mother's cooking pots. As they walked across the warming desert sand, Khuana and her grandmother took places behind, hoping no one would notice old Gaushe's limp. In spite of Khuana's gladness and optimism, the leg did not bend very far, no matter how much her grandmother exercised it. Gaushe walked with a limp, hiding her pain from Khuana. Khuana was happy because she knew they only had to walk until shadows were as long as themselves. Then they would all dig a hole and rest until nightfall. That would give her plenty of time to rub life back into the leg.

Before them moved the other twenty-nine members of the camp, strung out in single file upon the grayish-yellow sand as if they were connected by an invisible rope. Khuana could see her father near the head of the line with old Tsona. Her father, like all the men, wore only scanty clothes and the sun sparkled and gleamed upon his brown back. He carried only a bow over his left arm and a leather quill of arrows dangled down the center of his back.

Gishay, who was always ready to play, laughed and jumped. It was his first time to walk among the men on a long journey. He looked back several times, wrinkling his nose and waving, trying to get Khuana's attention. She waved back at him, though it was difficult with the cooking pots and the rolled gemsbok skin that she carried. Gishay, after being sure of Khuana's attention, began to swagger along, imitating first the walk of Kwi, whose feet were turned slightly in so that he walked like a dancing deer, and then old Tsona, who walked on his heels as if he were always killing ants. Gishay first pointed to the person he would imitate, then he imitated that person's walk. When he had finished imitating a person, he would wave to Khuana while he jumped up and down in the sand, laughing, his hand over his mouth so the older people wouldn't hear him. Then he imitated Nsue. Nsue always moved her head from side to side, turning her neck or moving her body with a little rhythm as though she heard music that nobody else heard. Khuana ran to catch up with Nsue.

"Look at silly Gishay," said Nsue. "Who is he imitating now?"

"It's you Nsue! Can't you see him moving his neck?"

"Silly," said Nsue.

Gishay, looking back at them and laughing, failed to see the small pile of sand until he tripped over it and lay on the ground. That at last was the thing that stopped his funny mimicry. Nsue and Khuana imitated his fall and Gishay laughed more than ever.

54

When they had first started out in the chill of the morning, the women and girls had worn their heavy robes of gemsbok, or chamois skin, that reached from their shoulders to the sand, but now as the sun climbed higher and higher, they began to take them off and carry them. In helping her grandmother fold her skin robe, Khuana caught a glimpse of her leg, and it set her heart beating wildly. The leg was swollen a bit and the site of the arrow wound bulged out in a blue mound.

Old Gaushe saw her watching. "Don't be so alarmed," she said. "The march is nearly over for the day."

Khuana said nothing but from that moment she was heavy with the knowledge that the wound would not heal unless her grandmother had medicine. She watched the shadows more closely now, and the brows of the marchers. They were beginning to sweat, but only slowly. Every step that her grandmother took was agonizing pain for her. Finally, Gaushe and Khuana fell far behind. Then Khuana saw old Tsona look back. They were amid low, parched brush and sand dunes. Tsona turned and signaled everyone to make skerms. The day's marching was over.

"We will stay here at the back of the line. Dig our hole here, Khuana," said Gaushe. But before Khuana could begin digging, her mother came back to them, carrying her fat baby brother who was asleep, his mouth still at her breast.

"What is the cause of your limp, mother?"

"Old age!" answered Gaushe, trying to laugh but only managing a grimace.

"You were as spry as a klipspringer yesterday. Everyone is saying you must have slipped and hurt yourself."

Khuana opened her mouth. She was going to tell her mother everything.

"Moth—" but old Gaushe put a finger to her lip.

"Ch . . . Ch . . . Ch . . ."

Khuana's mother saw the gesture. "So you two have got secrets. Well, I'm glad to see Khuana so fond of you and looking after you so well." Her words were like stabs in Khuana's body.

"Mother, it's my fault grandmother is badly hurt," she blurted out.

Her mother looked at her thoughtfully, then bent down beside Gaushe in the sand. "Here, let me see it."

Khuana's mother felt the old wrinkled limb that was hot with fever. She let her breath out sharply as she saw the puffy blue wound. Then, rising to her feet, she stared blankly at Khuana. Khuana looked from her mother to the wound on her grandmother's leg. The leg was now so swollen that the metal bangles on old Gaushe's leg cut into the flesh.

Her mother was running now, calling to her husband. "Kwi! Kwi! Come! You must come. Our old mother is very sick!"

Everybody seemed to come running at once. They stopped digging their holes and their short shadows fell around Gaushe.

"How did it happen?" several asked, but old Gaushe lay back in the sand, her wrinkled hands covering her eyes, breathing evenly but saying nothing.

Khuana's body shook with sobs as she saw her father carefully file off with a hard stone the bangles that her grandmother had put on her legs long before Khuana's mother was born. It was sad because a woman once married was given bangles by her husband and never afterwards removed them. Khuana and her mother rubbed Gaushe's leg, to keep the swelling down.

People went back to digging their holes in the sand, burrowing with cupped hands.

"Guess what old Mrs. Samgau said when she saw your grandmother's swollen leg?" cried Nsue, as she came running over to Khuana, dodging the flying sand. "She said, 'Poison! It looks like poison! If it isn't poison, I'll eat an ostrich,'

"Her hole is right next to ours, Khuana, and I overheard what she said."

Nsue was thoughtful for a minute. She glanced back at the adults. "Look Khuana, I wonder what old Tsona, your father, and the men are talking about. They've been like that for quite some time." Khuana didn't stop digging, but turned her head slightly in the direction of the men.

"I don't know," she said absently, but she was afraid that she did know.

"Khuana, was it poison?"

"Huh?"

"Was it poison like Mrs. Samgau said?"

Khuana looked at her best friend, her lips quivered, and she dug sand from beneath her fingernails. "Yes, an arrow slipped . . ."

"Oh, Khuana did you . . . did you? . . ."

"Yes, I did it. And I feel so miserable. So, don't condemn me, please! Don't hate me, Nsue! And do you know what the men are talking about now?" She threw a defiant look in their direction. "They are discussing how they can leave grandmother to the desert jackals," she burst out crying. "How can they leave her behind!"

"Oh . . ." said Nsue.

"But they'll never do it." Khuana scratched hard into the soil. "If they leave her, then they'll just have to leave me, Nsue." Khuana straightened up again and gently caught her friend's arm. "Nsue, you must promise not to tell."

"Khuana, they'll find out it was poison anyway."

"I'm not talking about that. I mean that I'll stay here with grandmother. Promise, Nsue."

"I promise! But they won't let you."

"They won't even know I've stayed," she said. "Don't tell. You promised." Khuana clenched her teeth as she dug, and the sand flew out behind her.

"I won't tell, Khuana! But . . . I don't want you to stay. Please don't stay."

7

Abandoned

Through the long, hot day, the Bushmen lay back in their cool burrows, the animal skins spread over them to keep out the sun's heat. The shadows of the nearby dunes lengthened eastward. They grew longer and longer until their bases flowered a reddish yellow, their peaks spattered purple over the sky, and the shadows moved on until darkness fell over them and became one immense shadow covering everything.

Then it began—silently: Khuana watched people creep from their holes. It was an ugly sight. All the loveliness and beauty had changed; instead of the early morning when it was good to roll from beneath the warm chamois, to hear chattering women, crying babies; to smell the first smoke of old Tsona's pipe and to be awake when the whole camp came alive with memories of the camp-fires and stories of the night before in front of them; instead of those good times, people crept from their burrows now, like night animals. They quietly stole away from their places as though they left something unpleasant there. Khuana lay there listening to the even breathing of old Gaushe. Even when her mother started folding the things and gave her the baby, Khuana's grandmother did not move. Khuana feared to ask old Gaushe about her leg. She knew what the answer would be.

While she sat there, old Tsona came with her father and, by lighted bunches of grass, looked at her grandmother's leg. Everybody else stayed away, preparing their things for travel. By the briefly lighted flare, Khuana looked anxiously at the men's faces, hoping she could read something there. How was the leg? Would it be all right? What were they going to do? If only their eyes would show some sign! If only they would say something! Surely they were not going to leave her? They couldn't! They couldn't leave her grandmother to die. Khuana pleaded silently with them in her mind.

When her father and old Tsona went away, still without speaking, Khuana at last looked at Gaushe. "You should get up and exercise your leg, grandmother. It's time to go."

"You mustn't worry about me, Khuana."

"Ask the sand not to cover the desert, old grandmother. How is the leg?"

"Stiff. I can't even move my toes this time."

"Try! Remember this morning you didn't think you would be able to walk."

"Look, my child, your father and old Tsona must do an unpleasant thing. Don't look so terrified! And don't make trouble for them. When the march stopped we had

60

fallen far behind. They could have gone farther today without me."

Khuana clung to her old grandmother's neck.

"There are thirty people out here. Think of the children. What they must do is to save everybody's life. Maybe I would only live to be but one rain older, anyway; but think of the babies, even this one you hold."

"But they won't leave you. They can't."

"They won't want to leave me, but I'm not going."

"But I won't go without you."

"The people are moving off."

"Come on, Khuana," she heard her mother call. Then the grown-up people already knew of the decision to leave grandmother behind. It was not a thing to be discussed or cried over. They would just leave her as if they expected her to walk back to the camp where surely there would be enough water to support one healthy person, but they knew in her condition she would not be able to live very long in the desert. Then her fate was to be the same fate as her husband's. But by leaving her, they would save the lives of all the others. It was all Khuana's fault. She kissed her grandmother and cried in her ear, "I'll be back. I'll never leave you, old grandmother."

Then they were off, marching in the cool darkness. Hot tears streamed down Khuana's cheeks and painful sobs wracked her youthful body. They marched off in the dusk and the huddled lonely figure of her grandmother blended with the darkness of the dunes as though only morning light would reform her like a shadow. No voice was heard, but several mournful sighs escaped her mother and Khuana felt better to think that someone else was

sad about it too. She went up to speak to her father, and though he had always been kind and thoughtful to her before, now he seemed cold as he told her harshly to get back with the women and children. She was ashamed to meet the eyes of Nsue or any of the others. She turned her head aside, but Nsue caught her hand and squeezed it as she passed.

"Don't worry. Grown-ups know best. I'm glad you didn't stay behind."

"Nsue, I have told you. I am staying with grandmother; I shall go back to her at the first chance I get. But you must not tell!"

Then Khuana realized Nsue was crying; she quickly pushed something into Khuana's hand and ran away up the line of people. Khuana realized it was Nsue's most prized possession—her tortoiseshell powder box.

Khuana took the last place in the line. She marched as they all did—in silence. Their feet on the sand made hardly any noise; only a sound like dry leaves rubbing together. She thought about the sand. She had to think of something to keep her from running away from the marchers and going back to her grandmother. She thought about how the sand burned her feet during the daytime and how cool it was to her toes in the early morning. She felt it now oozing between her toes and sinking and pulling her backward a little with each step forward. Where did the sand stop? The whole world seemed like cruel, shifting sand with nothing solid to hold on to. She had heard about hills leading into mountains —but where were they? Where did the sand stop?

They pressed on, a band of silent marchers in the silent desert night—walking, walking, all night. Khuana thought of this as a point in her favor. It could work to her advantage if she was patient enough. All she had to do was to walk along with them until they were used to her being at the back of the line. Then she could slip away and go back to her grandmother.

She waited until she had studied all the stars in one quarter of the sky. Then, as she heard no one speak or seek the intimate company of anyone else, she stopped, then waited. Finally, she turned, and after walking a short distance, ran and ran, wondering as she ran if some night animal had not already found the sick old woman.

Once, amid the heavy hammering of her heart, she stopped to listen and see if they were chasing her to bring her back, but the desert was silent. She ran on.

The light of the stars made the sandy desert a gray sea upon which her feet faltered and skimmed, and her toes splashed the sand about as if it were the foam of wave tips. When the earth began to sink and a high wavelike dune rose on her left, she knew she had neared the spot. The holes they had dug and lain in during the day were like yawning black pits in the desert as their color stood out from the grayness of the surface sand.

She found Gaushe resting in the burrow as they had left her. She had not even changed position.

"Don't be frightened. It's only me, old mother."

"I knew it would be you, Khuana." Old Gaushe pulled the child down beside her. "I knew you'd come back, but you shouldn't have."

"Why do you say that, grandmother? Everything will be fine."

"I say it because I can no longer look after you. Now it's you who are grown up and I the child." Neither of them spoke for a while. They sat on the side of the burrow, looking up at the stars.

"They will miss you and come looking."

"I marched at the end of the line and they are all so sick over having had to leave you that they don't smile, talk, or even look at one another. With luck they won't miss me until morning and they'll know then I'm one sleep away, too far to come searching. It would endanger the lives of all the rest. They will know I'm with you."

"Oh, Khuana, Khuana!" old Gaushe weakened at last. "I'm glad of you child, I thank Gao Na for giving me such a different daughter, one who loves me so. Yet I am afraid. Death to me means nothing, but now it's both of us against this." She stretched out her hands toward the desert.

Khuana's eyes sparkled with confidence as the stars played about in the skies. "Grandmother, I don't think about it in that way. You and me and Gao Na. That's good. We've got his mercy, your age and experience, and I'm young. You tell me what to do and I'll do it. If your leg can't walk, mine can run for you; if your eyes can't see I'll describe the thing to you. Then you give me your wisdom and we shall see."

Old Gaushe smiled and part of it bubbled into a laugh that was so full and happy it seemed youthful. Khuana was far happier here than she had been on the march.

"What should we do, grandmother?" Khuana asked after they had sat watching the stars until very late.

"That's a hard thing to decide, my child. I can't walk at all, but I could hobble or crawl back to that dried-up water hole—the place we left yesterday. With luck we could dig and suck enough water to last the two of us for about ten sleeps, but the moon has to be reborn and die again before the rains come. We couldn't find enough food back at the dried-out riverbed to feed us and I'm afraid that by the time the new moon came we wouldn't be alive to welcome it."

"And your leg? Don't forget it."

"I'm not forgetting. At the omuramba it is sure to get worse and if it does you will be left alone." She shuddered. "A horrible thought! No, the best thing would be to follow the dry river that we can cross before the night is finished, until we pass on into the hills near which we lost your grandfather. In one of the valleys we are sure to find water, and somewhere about there will be growing the herb medicine. We must find herbs to heal my leg."

"Let's do that, grandmother. We can get there. I'll carry you."

So taking nothing except a small cooking pot, a chamois skin, Khuana's bow and arrows, and Gaushe's water bag, they set out across the desert. Gaushe, leaning heavily on Khuana, was barely able to lift her sore leg, let alone bend it. They moved so slowly that Khuana reasoned they must be still near the burrows when a pale yellowish-purple light appeared on the eastern sand, and star-shaped dunes emerged from the night's darkness. Khuana and her grandmother were both tired, but as Gaushe had said the dry river could be reached before the night was finished, Khuana dared not stop until the river was in sight.

8

Two Against the Desert

The sun peeped its red eye over the eastern sands, then slowly pushed up its head until it was staring straight at the backs of the two thin figures upon the desert as they limped on. Finally the sand gave way to parched shrubs and brown grass.

Old Gaushe, her eyes closed against the pain of her leg, felt the crunch of leaves under her foot.

"We're near the dry river, Khuana, let's rest now."

"No, grandmother," Khuana said firmly. "I know you're tired, but just please keep going until we see the dry river—see the omuramba."

A few feet farther on there was a break in the level ground. About them the brown grass and shrubs were thick and soon they stood on the bank of the dried-up river. In places sand dunes occupied its bed. Long stretches of its hollowed floor were matted with dried-up dead plants and roots.

Khuana pulled roots aside and scooped out a cool cave

for her grandmother. After seeing her grandmother settled in, Khuana began looking for food. She saw a few tracks of rats and rabbits in the sand and searched along the riverbed for their burrows. But she saw none. Only the dried droppings. Then catching and pulling up roots, she searched among the dried-up brush of the banks, her arrow and bow ready. What luck it would be to find a kangaroo rat or a desert hare. But she saw neither of these. Finally she and her grandmother had to settle for some uncooked plant roots. They had not enough water to cook the roots so Khuana peeled them and they sat munching them.

Outside their cave the desert was sizzling hot. Khuana could see little waves of heat rising from the sand and brown grass. She hoped that the sun's heat would not set the dried grass afire until they had moved on. Each year while moving they had to avoid desert grass fires started by the sun's heat.

"Khuana," Gaushe said, thoughtfully, "I don't say this to complain but because you said that my wisdom and experience should guide us."

"Yes, grandmother?"

"I think it would be better if you took the water—well most of it—and set out for those hills alone. You . . ."

"Nonsense, grandmother, we're staying together."

"No. I didn't finish. It's only three sleeps away now. You're young and could get there easily. Then you could come back for me."

Khuana thought for a minute. Then she said, "How is your leg, grandmother? Will you not be able to move with the darkness?"

"I think not child. My leg is swollen even more."

Khuana uncovered the leg and jerked her head back. She thought at first it had an odor, but perhaps she'd been wrong, for she smelled nothing now. The wound was swollen and had a puffy bluish tinge. Khuana noticed with anxiety that now there were always gray desert flies flicking around the leg. She tore a piece of leather from the top of her chamois and wrapped it around the leg, covering the sore.

"No, grandmother, I'm not leaving you. The desert is so big and it is easy to get lost. So everywhere we go, we go together. I'll only leave you for a few minutes at a time when I must search for food."

Gaushe did not protest. The day wore on and not even desert butterflies could be seen moving in the heat. It was almost impossible to believe that in less than a month from now this desert grass and shrub would be succulent green. Five days after the first rains, the whole area around the river bed would be covered with fast blooming desert flowers, white daisies, and golden desert dandelions.

"Now we are only three sleeps away from the hills," said Khuana as they started walking at dusk that evening. This time the pace was much slower, for old Gaushe could hardly drag the leg. At the most they could go on for only one more sleep, Khuana thought to herself.

"Grandmother, I think I must carry you." Khuana bent to lift the old woman, but Gaushe protested firmly.

"No, child, we would never get there that way. You're our only hope; don't completely tire yourself."

By the middle of the night, when the North Star had begun to fade in preparation for the coming sun, they no longer stumbled over the roots of the riverbed. Old Gaushe grasped Khuana's arm.

"Wait a minute, child. Something is wrong."

"We're just on loose sand."

"Yes, that's it. There shouldn't be loose sand. This omuramba stretches all the way to those hills unless . . . unless . . . yes, perhaps that's it; it's just a sand drift covering a part of the bed." But the sand sloped upward and soon they were no longer in a riverbed but out upon the flat desert.

Old Gaushe sighed. "Now we have only the stars and sun to guide us. The river has been eaten by the desert."

"But couldn't it come out somewhere up ahead?"

"Let's walk on and see." They struggled on in silence. The first light rose to reveal sand and sand dunes, no plants and no riverbed.

"How far do you suppose we have come, grandmother?" Khuana asked when the sun rose.

"With my hobbling, only half a sleep, I am afraid."

Khuana decided to sacrifice the morning marching time to gathering food and searching for water. The reason for this was clear to her and she had thought of little else during the night. First she remembered how food was always easier to find in the desert grass after a fire. She had wanted to start a fire, but knew it was unsafe as long as her grandmother was in the dried brush and could not move fast enough to dodge into the desert. Now with the riverbed and brush buried deeply beneath piles of sandy drifts, and Gaushe safely out on the sand, she could race back to the riverbed and start a fire along its bank. She also knew that if she did not find water soon they would die of thirst. She reasoned that water would allow rest for a day, and with it she would cleanse her grandmother's wound with boiled water and salt. She looked again at the strip of leather tied around the wound. Slap! There were those nasty desert flies again. Slap! She got one that fell into the sand near the leg.

"Why are we stopping so early, Khuana?" Gaushe said, her voice full of gratefulness for the rest. Khuana stooped and began digging a burrow.

"Were there ever any water holes near here, old grandmother?"

"No, I never knew of one in the dry season. The nearest waterhole, if it is not as dry as it was in the year Samgau and the others died, is two and a half sleeps away."

Khuana helped her grandmother into the burrow and fastened over the chamois skin.

"You'll be all right there. I'm going to look for food and water."

"Go well," Gaushe said.

The coolness of the morning made movement easier. Khuana, moved by a sense of urgency, skimmed over the desert, covering the distance over the soft sand drift back to the riverbed in a short time. Soon dry blades of grass peeped through the layers of drifted sand, and after a few more steps she stood among the brush and shrubs they had walked over the night before.

It seemed to Khuana that everything to do with the real business of existence were "men's things": women were not supposed to make fires either. But Khuana, always a practical girl, had watched whenever she saw anyone in the camp perform a skill. So, unlike the other girls, she had learned to shoot an arrow as well as make a fire. She quickly found two dry sticks to make fire. Using an arrowhead from her kaross, but not the poisoned one, she bored a hole in one of the sticks and filled the hole with dry grass and a piece of dry rotting twig. Next she sharpened the point of the other stick. She placed this pointed stick into the hole of the first and began to twirl it back and forth between her hands.

She stopped after a few minutes, feeling the tinder in the hole of the stick. It was warm. That was better. She twirled it again and again. She was so bent on her work that her tongue poked out from the corner of her mouth. When she smelled smoke she increased the speed and the tinder burst into flames. She put on more grass and some branches she had found. The fire flared and crackled and the desert wind whipped and lashed it until it leapt like ferocious desert jackals at the nearby grass and bushes. In no time at all it raced across the desert, sending up smoke and throwing out coils of burnt blades. Khuana looked about on the desert for signs of animals trying to escape the burning grass. She thought she heard the cry of a bird, but when she looked all around, above the dancing flames, she did not see one. It must have been a sizzling, crackling branch of wood.

As the fire moved on, she took a stick and began digging in the soil around the trees for grubs. Then she looked in the nearby riverbed for lizards. She knew if they were there they would have burrowed deep into the sand. Looking up suddenly, she caught sight of something that looked like a burning bush whisking back and forth over the riverbed. She was about to look away again when her attention was caught and held by the lifelike

movements of the object. It let out several squeaks as it moved in long frantic hops toward Khuana. It was an animal. It scurried on by her and she saw that it was a jack rabbit, on fire. She smelled its scorching fur as it leapt out of the riverbed and hopped out across the sand.

Khuana crawled swiftly up the riverbank and chased the rabbit across the sand, carrying her digging stick in her hand. On and on the rabbit went squealing, rolling in the sand and keeping out of Khuana's reach. The sun was now hot and heat beat down against Khuana's flesh. Sweat trickled down her face and ran down her back. Her leather kaross swished against her skin. The rabbit ran across the desert in a kind of curve. Khuana lost all sense of direction. She only knew that the fire and river-bed were at her back. Then as she ran on she saw the smoke of the desert fire again, this time in front of her. She felt a dizziness, but kept going. She saw the rabbit slow down also, its fur no longer ablaze.

Slowly they made their way back to the riverbed. The rabbit did not go down into the riverbed but hopped along the bank. This time Khuana stopped to get her breath. The rabbit watched her now and with her first movements it ran off fast down the riverbank. If she could keep the rabbit between herself and the riverbank until they reached the burning brush, then she might have a chance to cut it off as it ran away from the fire, Khuana thought.

Gradually she increased her distance from the bank, making stamping sounds in the sand and striking her leg with the palm of her hand to urge the rabbit on. She was tiring again. Her lips were parched and dry. Her whole body was wet with sweat. Her back hurt and her head spun. As they neared the fire the smoke began to affect both Khuana and the rabbit. The rabbit pricked up its long ears in a frightened manner and ran erratically on the sand as if confused. Khuana rested and let it run around for a while until she thought it had become very tired, then she pretended to run in its direction. The rabbit tried to turn back along the riverbank, but it saw her blocking the way, and it ran out onto the open desert.

In front of it, now, lay the high sand dunes, like piles of sifted gold, glittering in the sunlight. The sun's rays smote the dunes into a shimmering blaze of fiery light that burnt and confused both rabbit and girl. The rabbit, caught between two fires, hesitated as Khuana gained on it. Then it began frantically to climb the dune, but at each hop the loose sand gave way and it whirled and rolled backward.

Khuana realized the rabbit was the only thing that lay between her and starvation. Climbing up on all fours, she brought the stick down on its head, stunning it. Catching her breath and breathing hard, she hit again and again until the singed furry mass lay lifeless and bloody upon the sparkling sand.

By this time Khuana was too sick to care. Her head spun faster and faster. She saw herself bending over to pick up the rabbit, then felt herself falling. A sick feeling hit the pit of her stomach and she rolled over upon the sand.

She lay almost lifeless, covered only by her leather chamois skin and kaross. The sun went down in the desert as a blaze of fire and she still did not move. Night came on and desert ants, sensing the rabbit's blood, came out of the deep sand, covering the rabbit and her arm. It was only then that Khuana, without moving the rest of her body or opening her eyes, began to brush the ants from her hands. At first her movements were slow, but eventually they became faster. Gradually she opened her eyes and tried to sit up, still brushing away the ants, which were now crawling over her body, biting her. She rolled in the sand to get them off. Then she remembered where she was and knew what must have happened. Soon her eyes became accustomed to the darkness around her. She found the rabbit and got rid of the ants by brushing it and turning it over and over in the sand.

9

Lost

She remembered, with a shock, her grandmother sitting in the burrow worrying about her. She had waited all day without food or water. Khuana started off on unsteady legs for the riverbed. She would know it when she arrived because of the burnt grass around it. She walked for some time without reaching it.

She decided it must be in the direction opposite to the dune. She walked in that direction but only stumbled over the sand, never reaching any spot that she knew. Now, through the numbness, pain, and sickness of the day, Khuana's feet were uneasy, and though she had been unconscious most of the day, her limbs felt stiff and tired and she felt herself yawning and constantly closing her eyes while walking. She woke up with a start. She was frightened because she began to realize for the first time some of her problems; these were not separate but jumbled and mixed as though she were having a silly dream.

First she could see herself lost among zebras; a herd of zebras that knew how to smell water. Then she heard, though she could not see, her grandmother calling: "Lie still. Rest and sleep. Lie down near those ostrich eggs," and all around her on the sand were thousands of big ostrich eggs. "Don't worry about water, the zebras will find it for you."

Khuana fought against this giddy feeling. She dropped to her knees in a careful manner as if she feared to break the eggs. She would sleep—just for a while. Sleep! Then she would get up and go on. "Very tired," she heard herself say. "Need rest to think." She was lying with her head against an egg when she felt a sharp burning on her flesh. She leaped up, wide awake! In her sleepy wandering she had stumbled into the burning riverbed and had sat down on some hot rocks. "It almost had me," she murmured. "This desert is treacherous." That's what old Tsona meant when he said that anything could happen to a person alone in the desert, no matter how healthy or strong. The desert was a natural enemy of man and you had to be constantly on guard against it or it would stalk and slay you.

She took three deep breaths, regained some of her balance and clearness, then set off at a rapid pace toward where she thought she had left her grandmother in the desert. On the way, she stumbled over some dried sticks that had partly escaped the fire. She picked them up.

Khuana did not easily find the spot where she had left her grandmother. At first she was too stiff and drowsy to move with great speed, but as the night grew cooler and the slow, cold desert wind came up she felt fresher and moved faster. The stars were bright but as yet the moon had not risen, so it was not easy to see distinct objects upon the desert.

Arriving at what she thought was the spot where she had left her grandmother, she cupped her hands around her mouth and called, "Morro, grandmother, Morro." There was no answer except the soft sighing of the wind and the whispering of sand drifting by. "I hope the sand hasn't covered her," Khuana thought anxiously, walking on.

Then, against a sandy incline, she saw the chamois skin spread over the burrow. Khuana's heart leapt up with gladness. She had found her grandmother again. Now at least part of their problem was finished; they were together again. They had a rabbit they could roast and a little water to drink, perhaps enough to last them for another day. Khuana still felt a little dizzy, but it didn't matter. Now she would be able to sleep and rest, and then her grandmother could help her think what to do next.

Khuana went up to the burrow and pulled back the chamois skin. She pushed the rabbit forward. "Look old grandmother, I'm back and I've got a rab—" But she spoke only to the empty hole. The burrow was empty, her grandmother nowhere in sight.

Khuana felt around inside the hole, her mouth open, her breath coming in gasps. She turned over the chamois skin as if she expected to find Gaushe there. She looked up and over the surrounding desert and even glanced up at the stars. Then she yelled: "Grandmother! Grandmother! Oh, dear old grandmother, where are you? Where are you?"

Her voice rose high with sorrow and weeping. Her body shook with sobs and her voice rang out through the empty desert. Bright tears welled up in her eyes. Perhaps, perhaps, she thought, animals had dragged her grandmother from the burrow. But there would be signs of a struggle, tracks, or even blood in the sand. She looked about frantically. There was nothing.

Khuana finally sat down, reasonably calm after she had stopped crying. "I can't find her in the night, I am too tired myself. I would wander away and get lost as I did at the fire. What I should do is get some rest and be ready to look for her with the first light of morning."

She climbed into the burrow and was surprised to find the water bag and her grandmother's kaross still there. She was very thirsty and drank two mouthfuls of water. She pulled the chamois skin around her. Even then she fought against sleep, for it seemed that if only she could think about it a while the kaross and the water bag held a message that could somehow tell her what had happened to her grandmother. But it was cold out and she couldn't stay awake, couldn't keep her eyes open. They kept closing . . . closing . . . closing . . . and she fell back into the open arms of the desert, into a deep slumber.

With the first light of morning Khuana jumped up, startled. She felt as if she were being watched and glanced around. But all she saw was the clean sweep of the open desert. The sky was blue and clear as happens in the dry season, and blue met with white sand. To her left there was flat sand for some distance, ending in a star-shaped dune.

Khuana could not think how or why her grandmother had disappeared. She only knew the old woman must be somewhere near this burrow or up ahead. How could she walk off when her leg pained her so? And today it would probably be worse. The whole thing was difficult to understand, unless her grandmother had been crazed with pain and hunger. She lifted the water bag. She couldn't be sure but she felt that with the exception of the two swallows she had herself drunk before falling asleep last night, no water had been taken from the bag. But why take off her kaross and leave it? A thought came to Khuana as she gazed over the desert and she smiled. Could it be true? Yes! It was the only possible answer. Khuana said softly to the sand dune, "You naughty, old, sweet grandmother." She jumped up and ran to the dune as fast as she could. She stopped once or twice to look for tracks but she saw none. The drifting sand would have covered them anyway. She climbed the dune, sinking down in the sand to her ankles. When she stood on the top and could look downhill on the other side, there, lying in a heap, she saw her grandmother.

Khuana ran shouting to her, thinking she might be too late. She feared that the heat of yesterday and the cold of night, hunger, pain, and thirst had already done their job, and already defeated her. When she dropped beside the old woman, she could hardly see if her grandmother was breathing—because of her own pounding heart and fast breathing. Then the eyelids fluttered and opened in the sweet, wrinkled face and Khuana swept up her grandmother into her arms.

"Grandmother, you sweet, old naughty grandmother. You tried to leave me alone in the desert. I knew it the moment I saw the water and your kaross."

Tears ran down the wrinkled cheeks and Khuana was crying, her face close to Gaushe's. Their hot tears met and old Gaushe's weak arms hugged her granddaughter.

"Forgive me, child, but I'm so weak, such a burden. You could do much better alone. You could reach those hills in a day without me."

"Get to those hills? Then what would I do alone? You're wrong, grandmother. I was without you yesterday and I got lost. I was sick, out of my head, and couldn't find my way back here. Oh, how could I find my way to hills which I last went to when I was a child of six years old. Grandmother, we can only get to the waterholes if we stay together."

Old Gaushe rubbed Khuana's head.

"My child, I'll never leave you alone again upon the desert."

"Oh, grandmother, let's go."

Back at the burrow Khuana roasted the rabbit while her grandmother talked about past Bushmen camps and dances. In spite of herself, Khuana dropped a tear on the sand.

"I wonder what is the first thing they'll do when they get to Guatscha pan," she said.

It was the first time she had felt a yearning to be back with the Bushmen band. She thought of Nsue and funny Gishay. Her nose wrinkled in a smile when she remembered her fat baby brother. She wished they were safe at camp again, listening to the stories of Cripple Guike. Even the company of old Mrs. Samgau did not seem so bad now that she missed them all so.

"Well, when they arrive, they'll meet your uncle Nku and aunt Mtati. They'll say *Morro* all around. There'll be plenty of water and a feast at night, with a big fire. And, of course, a moon dance when the new moon comes. But I am afraid our absence will sadden them a bit."

Khuana and Gaushe were silent for a moment, listening to the meat sizzle on the fire, its juice running out. The smell made the mouth and stomach eager to taste it.

"Don't cook it too long, Khuana, you'll cook away all the water."

Khuana smiled. "I'm hungry too, grandmother."

She pulled off a hind leg and passed it to Gaushe. "Let them feast at Guatscha pan. We'll have a feast here in the open desert."

Old Gaushe bit into the meat; the juice ran down her chin and her eyes smiled.

"Who knows! They may get to Guatscha pan only a day or two before we get there."

"Do you suppose they looked for me, old grandmother?"

"I'm sure they wanted to look for you. They would know you came back to join me, but they wouldn't know where to look for us."

"Anyway, I hope father didn't look. We are better off here together, grandmother. Sooner or later they would have been angry with me because I like to hunt and do men's jobs."

Old Gaushe laughed as she ate. "Sooner or later," she said.

The sun was up when they finished eating, put away the rest of the rabbit in Khuana's kaross, and had a drink of water.

Khuana helped old Gaushe to her feet and they moved out across the desert. Perhaps it was because they'd just eaten but the sun seemed ferociously hot. It was behind them and struck like hot pellets on their backs and heads. Before they had gone far they were both sweating. They stopped when they could bear it no longer and Khuana dug a burrow big enough for both of them.

"We'll get plenty of rest today, grandmother, for we must start at sundown. Our water will not last us through another day."

Sundown saw them on their way again. Khuana was nearly carrying Gaushe, for the swelling of her wound had now come up to her knee. Khuana felt sick each time she remembered what she had seen when she looked at the wound while her grandmother slept. She had pulled back the chamois skin. The piece of leather from her kaross no longer covered the wound, and it gave off a decaying odor like rotted meat. Small gray desert flies still flicked about it, droning. The wound was open and while she looked at it, a small white drop fell from it onto the sand. She thought the sore was draining and took it to be pus dropping out, but there was something in the way the drop moved or rather twisted that caught her eye and made her look closer at it. It was alive! A worm! A maggot! She was very frightened. Now, every time she thought of it, she felt sick. Only her will pushed her onward over the sand with her heavy load.

The stars came out, shone, and performed their movements across the sky. At times, Khuana had the odd sensation that the desert was the sky and they walked upside down on it. Toward morning, old Gaushe groaned with every step and Khuana could hardly move because of her grandmother's weight. But she knew to stop meant time lost, and perhaps they would be unable to start again.

With the first light of morning, a strange and pathetic thing happened. Khuana, looking ahead, seemed to recognize the place. The sand was low with little ridges and now the light faced them. But that was impossible! The sun should come from the opposite direction! Then as she looked closer, she saw a sand dune on her left. It was star-shaped. She stopped still and asked her grandmother to rest for a moment. Khuana ran on ahead and climbed to the top of the dune. Looking over the other side she saw, as she had expected, her grandmother's burrow of a day before, where they'd eaten the rabbit. They had walked all night—in a circle! Khuana had been too tired to watch the stars carefully. She could have sat down and wept. But she couldn't let her grandmother know how hopeless everything seemed. She stood there a moment, fighting the urge to cry. Finally she regained control of herself. She went back, gave her grandmother a piece of rabbit, took the last piece herself and sat in silence. When they had finished she said, "We travel in sunlight today, grandmother. We travel all through the day until we can no longer stand it."

They moved off again, the rising sun on their backs. It was fear that drove Khuana and Gaushe on and on across the desert that day. Khuana resolved not to stop until they both dropped on the desert. They went as though the sun were some devil's eye burning their backs and they fled from it in panic. Gaushe limped with a firmer, more determined step in spite of the condition of her leg. And they made good progress. Probably their strength increased because they were desperate. Whatever it was, it drove them through the searing heat of day. They kept nothing back for the next day. With water and food gone, this was the only day they were sure of. Tomorrow they might not be alive.

The land changed under their feet from sand to a white dust, then to a flat area of solid white. The wind blew dust across Khuana's face and into her mouth and she was surprised to find it tasted salty.

Here the sun was worse. It struck the white salt and flashed back into the eyes and against the skin. Where the hot earth was whitest the sun's glare blinded them. Old Gaushe panted with thirst and fatigue.

"We've done enough for now," she said between gasps. "Nobody can stay alive upon this salt flat for long. If we find a rock or any kind of shelter we should stop."

But there were no rocks and no shelters and by mid-day they lay upon the salt flats weak, drained of water, and crazed with thirst and fatigue. Khuana instinctively tried to dig a hole but the salt was hard under her finger-nails, breaking the skin, causing the blood to flow, and stinging her.

Looking about in front of them, old Gaushe saw a wide crack in the earth. "Let's crawl in there, Khuana." It was not very deep, nor comfortable, but they lay in it for the remainder of the day covered with the chamois skin.

Even when the cool evening came neither of them moved. They were almost without hope. Sometime in the evening, Khuana said:

"You know, old grandmother, we were lost last night." Old Gaushe grunted.

"I didn't want to tell you then, but we went in a circle all night and came back to the place where I lost you, near that star-shaped dune."

"I knew it," said Gaushe.

"You did?" said Khuana with surprise.

"I don't want you to raise your hopes too high, Khuana, but I think we are near water."

"Near water! How do you know, grandmother?"

"Maybe I can smell it. I can't tell exactly. Perhaps I'm light in the head."

"I'm so thirsty I could die." Khuana's lips were cracked and her mouth dry. Her whole skin was parched an unhealthy gray. The gray salt was also on Gaushe's face and arms. As they pulled themselves upright, there was a great flutter over their heads; Khuana ducked back down.

"What was that?"

"An owl! I think."

They climbed out of the hole and followed in the direction of the disappearing sun. Toward dusk old Gaushe pointed to a grasshopper upon the salt flats.

"Is that a sign of water nearby?" Khuana asked.

"Either that or the rains have begun in the north. But I think if the rains had started there would be many grasshoppers, not just one."

The earth now had more cracks and the land sloped up toward the south.

"Khuana, if we find water," her grandmother said, "please don't drink until I have seen it."

"Yes, grandmother. But why?"

Her grandmother did not answer. "Please don't drink," Gaushe repeated.

It was Khuana who, raising her head from the desert floor a little while later, saw a tiny brown and white butterfly through the grayish-yellow mist that hung around it. At first she thought it was one of those dream images

88

that people see when they have been out on the desert too long without water.

"Look grandmother! Look!"

Old Gaushe raised her head and recognition beamed in her eyes.

"I know this place," she said. "But where are the big flat hills? They should be straight ahead."

Then they both saw the image of the big flat-topped rocky hills just before the last light disappeared. But only for an instant, then the hills were shrouded in darkness.

"There was a water hole . . ." said old Gaushe, lifting some of her weight from Khuana's shoulder. She almost fell.

They noticed then that the ground beneath them began to slope downward and beneath their feet were small hard pebbles. Some pebbles rolled down the slope at the touch of their feet and soon they heard splashes. The pebbles were falling into water. Khuana and Gaushe stopped. They heard the splash again. Old Gaushe said, "Ah!" It was a sigh of relief.

When her feet touched the water, still warm from the day's heat, Khuana's first impulse was to stoop and drink, to fall down into the water and let her whole body drink. But she remembered her grandmother's warning. She stood in the darkness licking her parched cracked lips, while Gaushe touched her finger to the water and tasted it.

"Uh, it's salty!" she said. "We can't drink this. It would kill us."

Beside her, Khuana began to moan. "Can't we have just a swallow?"

"No need to worry, Khuana, there must be other water nearby."

They searched until they were almost in the shadow of a tall flat hill. There they stumbled into a low area and at once old Gaushe pointed the way to a water hole. When they reached it, immediately they both fell on their faces and drank. They drank until they were breathless; and while catching their breaths they splashed water on their faces, in their hair, down their backs, and all the while they laughed. They couldn't stop laughing. Then they lay in the water, and old Gaushe said, "Ah! Ah!" a thousand times.

Later they sat with their backs against some rocks in front of a fire. Khuana had made the fire because they had heard lionlike noises in the distance, and the fire would keep wild animals at bay. Then Khuana said, "There ought to be a dance tonight, grandmother. If I had my guashi, how I would play and never go to sleep."

She hummed a tune, one of those sung in the camp during the moon dance. In the middle of the tune, Khuana suddenly stopped. She went up to her grandmother and touched her tenderly.

"Please excuse me, dear old grandmother. I'm so happy tonight I took no thought of your leg."

"Water was the first thing to worry about, Khuana, but the leg still pains me."

That could mean anything, Khuana thought. Her grandmother wouldn't complain. She felt the leg, and looked at it, but could not see it clearly by the firelight. "Wait until morning," Gaushe said.

"Well, the first thing in the morning, I'm going to look at it and we will go and search for your healing herbs in one of the canyons about here. With so much water there are bound to be plants growing here."

"There are likely to be dangerous animals here also. Didn't you hear those animal noises?"

"If there are animals, then we shall have food. I'll use my bow and poisoned arrows."

Old Gaushe laughed and her eyes sparkled over the fire.

"Silly girl, you are like leopard's teeth; you never give up once you have taken grip."

They slept soundly and more comfortably that night because they had found water. They felt sure they would find some kind of food and there was hope they might be able to do something for Gaushe's leg. Had she known, however, what sat nearby, Khuana would have kept her arrows and bow ready and she would never have gone to sleep so quickly that night.

10

Ostriches

The sun was striking the cliffs of the canyon before hunger and light nudged them awake, Khuana rolled from beneath the chamois blanket where she had slept with her grandmother. She went to the nearby water hole to wash her face and have a drink. She was still not wide awake, but when she had drunk and was raising her head from the water she saw a sight that made her angry with herself for sleeping so late. She knew that Bushmen never went to a water hole before sunrise unless they wanted to shoot an animal for meat. Now why was it, this morning of all mornings, she had slept past the animals' watering time? She knew the animals had already drunk because there in the soft earth all around the water were the tracks of animals. She circled the water hole, identifying them.

Those were the soft pads of a cheetah, these the rabbit, and there were the split hoofprints of an antelope, maybe a gemsbok. There was also the smooth slithering track where a snake had gone into the water hole, and a track on the opposite side where the snake came out. Bird tracks marked the mud all around the water hole. Then before she had completed the circle her heart beat wildly. Those tracks . . . they were like . . . they must be ostriches. She went back to help her grandmother down to the pool.

"Grandmother, what kind of tracks are these?"

"Here's where a lizard came down," she said, moving around the water hole in Khuana's direction. "These round hooves must be zebra. And below this soil—I can see where he went in—is the spade-footed toad."

Khuana's grandmother knew quite a bit about desert life and at any other time Khuana would have been interested, but now she cried.

"Not those, grandmother, these." She pointed.

A smile spread over old Gaushe's face. "Those could be of a big bird."

"A bird that can't fly, old grandmother?"

"Yes, that has eggs as big as one's head," said old Gaushe.

"And from the shells water canteens are made."

"The eggs are also good to eat," her grandmother teased.

"Oh grandmother," Khuana hugged her neck. "I knew they were ostrich tracks."

"You silly child, surely what we need most now is meat. Rabbits taste better than ostriches and are far easier to catch."

"For meat I'll try to catch the first thing I see, but I'll be thinking and planning for the ostrich all the time. As soon as I find meat, we will look for medicine for your leg."

93

"My leg still pains me, but it's better. Before you go hunting, I want to bathe it in that salt water. Maybe that will take away the swelling."

They had no difficulty finding the salty water hole but it was a great distance away. Gaushe told Khuana salt flats like this were found all around these hills and nearby there were several fresh-water holes. This was the range or territory of their band and no other Bushmen came this way. It had been seven dry seasons since some of their men had died for lack of water—that long dry season when they'd found all the water holes dry and not an animal anywhere in sight. Ever after, Tsona was afraid of repeating old Samgau's mistake, and so he never led the band this way. Each dry season he promised to send several men to look at the place during the next wet season. But when the rains came there was always so much food and happiness that he always forgot, until it was dry again. Then it was too late. This had happened before they had set out this time. Gaushe sighed. "Six seasons have made a big difference to the place. Now there is plenty of water, even near the end of the dry season. And there are lots of animals."

Khuana had put off looking at her grandmother's sore leg, because she dreaded what she might see. She remembered only too well the gray desert flies and the worms that fell out of it. So it was with a heavy heart that she sat her grandmother at the edge of the water with her leg dangling in the pool. When she unwrapped the bandage, she was surprised to see that the wound was clean. There was no rotting sore and there was no odor. But the leg was still swollen.

Khuana looked questioningly at old Gaushe. "The flies

and maggots did it," Gaushe said. "I have seen wounds they've cleaned before—ate all of the rotten sore and flesh away. But when they got into mine that first day, and I felt them wriggling, it made me sick inside. I really gave up hope then. It was you who made me go on. The next day the wound was no worse than the day before, and I thought that if I could bear it without you seeing them it might be all for the best, and the wound would get better. Now if we can get rid of the swelling and pain it will be fine. This salt water should drive that away and start the healing."

Khuana's eyes smiled and her heart jumped with gladness. She cupped her two hands together for water and splashed it on the leg and in the sore. Old Gaushe winced when the salt first struck the sore and shivered a little bit, but after that she lay enjoying the pressure of Khuana's hand on the swollen leg.

When Khuana had completed the task and they were again back at the rocks where they had camped and slept the night before, Khuana took her bow and pulled out the arrows and reeds from her kaross. She said, "Let's go hunting, grandmother."

So they both left the rocks of their camp and went searching in the valleys between the hills. In the valley the white earth gave way to sand and rocks. Grasses sprang up amid the sand and small green shrubs clung to the sides of the hill and in small clusters on the valley floor. Old Gaushe pointed out to Khuana several good cooking roots and they gathered dry pieces of wood for fire. Khuana saw several birds perched on a bush. She tried to bring one of them down with her arrow but she missed and they all flew off.

95

Then they came to a place where the earth was cracked and rocks were strewn all about. Khuana looked about under the rocks, hoping to surprise a rabbit or jerboa, but she saw nothing.

"Let's cook these roots today and we can go down to the water hole early in the morning to shoot meat," said her grandmother.

Khuana was about to agree when she climbed the pile of rocks and looked over onto a wide stretch of sand with occasional boulders popping out of the ground.

"Look, old grandmother. What's that?" Khuana ran down and helped her grandmother up the rock.

"They look like zebras," Gaushe said, shielding her eyes against the sun. "But what is that closer, in the sand, near those boulders?"

"I see a large animal moving there," said Khuana. "Maybe it's a gemsbok. If you stay here and watch, I'll try to creep around those boulders and get closer. If I succeed, we shall have gemsbok meat for supper."

It was a long walk for Khuana, moving upon the sand, around the boulders. There was a rising excitement in her breast because she felt if they got food, they could regain their strength and reach Guatscha pan. If she had enough time, she would have the thing she wanted most—an ostrich eggshell canteen. She did not think of the danger of her venture. She had heard that a good hunter always shot his arrow accurately, watched it strike home, then lay down in the sand to rest while the animal tried running away. The poison did the rest of the work. Finally, when the hunter had given the poison time to work, he got up and tracked the animal to where it had fallen.

Moving stealthily across the desert in this bent, crouching position—the sun on her neck, the hot sand burning her feet with every step, her bow fitted with a poisoned arrow—Khuana was unmindful of any danger or any resistance the gemsbok might put up.

She circled around behind the boulders and crept closer. Then she could see the creature she sought was not alone—there were two of them! A quick gasp escaped from Khuana's lips, for they were not gemsbok, but ostriches! There were two of them! She could hardly believe her good fortune. One of the ostriches walked about with its neck stretched and head high as though it scented danger. Its black body feathers and grayish-pink neck made a fine, proud sight moving over the ground. The other ostrich sat in the sand, its neck stretched out near the ground. Now Khuana could understand why the

sitting one couldn't be seen from where she and her grandmother had been watching. She had not seen the ostrich because the coat of the sitting one was gray and blended so perfectly with the sand that it was not easy to see it until it moved.

Khuana noticed that the standing bird was large and much taller than herself. She shook her head in wonder at their immense size and she marveled at their beauty. But the neck frightened her. It stretched long and sinister like an ugly snake searching for prey. While Khuana watched, it uttered two loud and frightful warning sounds. The sounds seemed to come from deep inside the ostrich and they jarred like the sound of a lion's roar. Khuana was afraid and would have retreated back across the desert, but she never got the chance. The great birds were still some distance away from the boulders, but the standing ostrich was looking carefully at the boulder behind which Khuana was hiding. The bird moved a few quick steps in that direction stretching its neck, giving Khuana the impression that it stood on tiptoe. It was amazing how few steps it took to cover the distance. What a long stride it had!

11

The Fight

Khuana lay very still behind the boulders. She dared not breathe. Until now she had never feared an ostrich. Perhaps it was because all the ones she had seen before were running away in the distance across the desert, and whenever ostriches were brought into camp by her father and other men they were already dead and looked like giant plucked chickens.

But this great ostrich, moving near her, its head in the air and the *sii . . . sii . . . sii . . . sissing* sounds escaping from its beak, and its black eyes which seemed to look straight through the rocks at her, was different altogether. She wanted to leave her place behind the rock and run away, but she forced herself to stay.

Drawing on her courage, she fitted an arrow to the bow, raised her body cautiously, and took aim at the ostrich. The big bird saw her and at once moved around the rock, coming straight for her. It tried to get close where it would be able to use its deadly feet to kick her.

But Khuana was quick; she took aim and fired an arrow at the thick middle part of the ostrich's body. The ostrich saw the arrow coming and lifted its arm-like wing. The arrow bounced off its feathers.

Khuana quickly searched among the boulders for shelter. Three boulders leaning together formed a small hole. Khuana, fearing snakes and lizards, but fearing the ostrich more, bent down and hurriedly squeezed and burrowed her way into the small hole. Inside, the shelter was quite large, and just as she turned and drew in her legs the ostrich's beak shot like a spear through the entrance. The bird pecked the sandy floor of the little cave, trying to reach her. Khuana, with fast beating heart, squeezed herself as close as possible to the opposite wall.

The ostrich's head did not remain inside for long. It was withdrawn and then shot in ferociously again several times. But the ostrich could not touch her. Then the beak disappeared. Khuana was afraid to move. Inside her small boxlike cave it was cool, though rays of sunlight peered through three or four small holes.

Khuana looked around the cave. Hanging from the wall of one rock, near Khuana's head, were several young naked bats. They moved only slightly and hung on the wall as if they had been glued on, and now and then they moved with the wind. On the ground under one corner of the boulder was a purple and red lizard.

Khuana was surprised to see one ray of light disappear from the cave. She looked closer for the hole through which the light had come. She saw an eye of the ostrich watching her. The eye was withdrawn. Light came in again, then the light was cut off and the ostrich's beak came in, fast! The hole was too small for the large head so only part of the beak came in. Khuana felt better when she found out that the ostrich could not get her. But then she could not attack the ostrich with her arrows either.

In the meantime, she didn't like being in the cave with the bats and the lizards. She had dropped her bow somewhere outside while escaping into the cave. She still had an arrowhead and a reed in her kaross.

Khuana sat there a while, thinking. While the ostrich was circling the rocks, maybe she could crawl out of the entrance, find her bow, then get back inside. She would try it!

She moved from the back of the cave, but she met the ostrich's beak poking in at the entrance and hissing like an angry snake. Khuana, frightened and defenseless without her bow, retreated back against the wall. She took her last arrow from inside the kaross that hung around her neck and fitted it to a hollow reed, also from her kaross. She waited tensely for the head to poke into the cave again. But it did not come. She waited and waited but no head came and the hissing noise was not heard again. Perhaps the ostrich had gone back to its nest. The moving shadows thrown by the rays of light entering the cave told Khuana the sun was almost down.

She took a chance and crawled to the entrance of the cave. She heard not a sound. She crawled all the way outside, looking left and right for her bow. She found it a short distance from the entrance. Cautiously she surveyed her surroundings; she looked toward the spot where she had first seen the ostriches. Their grayish outlines were barely visible against the sand and rocks but they were still there. She wanted to shoot one of them but she was still frightened from her last encounter. "Besides," she told herself, "grandmother will be worried."

She arrived back to find old Gaushe boiling roots and washing berries that she had gathered for their supper. The night came on fast, cool, and pleasant. Not yet fully rested from their long desert journey, Khuana and her grandmother ate and soon fell asleep.

Old Gaushe, chilled by the cool night and bothered by her sore leg, did not sleep well. She kept watch all night. When she saw the first bright slashes of daylight peeping through the eastern curtain of the sky, she gently shook Khuana awake.

"Khuana, the water hole, remember we must be there early enough to get meat for food. The animals come very early," whispered old Gaushe.

Khuana and Gaushe set out before it was fully daylight, and finding themselves a spot to hide behind some bushes just above the high rocks, they sat down to wait. Khuana had brought her bow but not her arrows. She cut several light sticks and made them into arrows by sharpening one end.

They didn't have to wait long before they heard the cough of a leopard. Khuana thought perhaps she should have brought her poisoned arrows after all. Already several birds were bathing; they were ducking their heads, breaking the night film, throwing arcs of ripples in the cool bright water.

The leopard's paw made a great swipe and feathers floated above the water, danced in a little breeze, and settled on the water. The bird was pinned beneath the leopard's paws. Khuana and old Gaushe watched while the leopard bit into the bird and then laid it aside while it had a drink. Having drunk, it took the bird away in its mouth.

While the leopard was still in sight, Khuana and Gaushe heard movements in the bush and on the sand. Small rodents, rats, and rabbits came into sight. Khuana let them drink; then, taking careful aim, she sent an arrow straight at a rabbit and killed it. The rabbit dropped onto the sand. The other rabbits did not even stop their drinking.

Khuana took aim again, but this time her pointed stick plopped into the sand. She tried for a guinea fowl with the next shot and aimed at the bulky body as though it were an ostrich. She hit it and it flipped about on the sand with the arrow sticking through its thigh. "That will be enough for our stomachs," Khuana said to herself.

Soon after they got back to camp Gaushe began to roast meat, but Khuana wanted to go looking for the ostriches.

"But there are two of them," said old Gaushe.

"I'll only shoot one. I've got only one arrow," Khuana explained.

"Then you won't get any eggs," said Gaushe. "The other one will see to that unless . . ."

"Unless what, old grandmother?"

"Unless you use your head."

"I will. I'll shoot one, then chase the other away from the nest with stones."

"Perhaps," said old Gaushe, with a twinkle in her eye, "but one seemed to have made *you* run to the stones before the last sleep. You know they often take turns sitting on the eggs. If you watched them until one went away for food, you'd have a better chance. Tell me, had she started to sit on the eggs?"

"One was sitting on the nest with her neck stretched out long."

"Was there an egg outside the nest?" asked Gaushe.

"I didn't see one."

"Then they are not yet sitting on the eggs. You watch them until one or maybe both of them go away for food, then you must be quick for they only go away for a short time."

When Khuana got to the boulders from which she could watch the ostriches, one ostrich was striding back toward the nest from the direction of the water hole.

"He's been to drink," thought Khuana. "Now, if the other one is thirsty it will go away to drink also." But both ostriches grazed near the eggs, pulling at grass and bushes.

The sun was overhead before Khuana saw both ostriches moving across the desert toward the water hole. By that time she was quite hungry. She waited until both ostriches had disappeared behind the rocks. Then she dashed as fast as she could to the nest, hurriedly scooped up two of the big eggs, and filled her kaross with them. The eggs were heavy to lift and each was almost as big as the head of a baby. The shells were very hard and firm.

Khuana had gone a good way from the nest when she saw one of the ostriches returning. The ostrich saw her at the same time. The bird gave a roar like a lion and began galloping like a big two-legged donkey straight for Khuana. Khuana could tell it was the cock by its black feathers and deep voice. Her heart beat faster and sweat stood out on her forehead. The ostrich, running across the barren land at a gallop, headed straight for her.

When she tried to run, she discovered the eggs were even heavier than she thought them to be. Carrying them it would be impossible for her to escape the galloping ostrich. She could not run properly. She stopped short, looking around for a place to hide. There was nowhere in sight except the rocks where she had hidden the day before. The ostrich gave another roar and his speed was such that it seemed to Khuana he would soar into the air and fly. She ran for the rock cave. Despite the speed of the ostrich, it still was quick enough to veer and turn its body, trying to cut her off. It was far from easy to run, even that short distance, carrying the heavy eggs and her bow and arrows. Perhaps if she dropped an egg it would distract the ostrich and slow him down. Khuana laid down one egg and kept running. The ostrich, bent on tearing her apart, didn't even notice the egg. Khuana had merely wasted her time in bending down to drop the egg.

Khuana just reached the cave, fell down on her knees, and crawled into it when the bird caught a piece of her gemsbok skirt and pulled her with great force against the entrance wall. Khuana quickly pulled the kaross strap from around her neck and pushed the egg out of the ostrich's reach.

The ostrich, still pulling on her skirt, was making the kaross pull against her neck, almost strangling her. The giant bird would probably have continued had it not seen Khuana's leg. It let go of the skirt long enough to stab at her leg with his beak. The wound made Khuana wild with pain. She jerked back her leg and pulled in her skirt at the same time. As she did so one of the holes was blacked out and an angry ostrich's eye peered at her and a *"sis-ssiss"* sound came in through the crack.

She realized the ostrich would not give up this time. It knew the egg was inside the cave and would wait for her, then try to pick her out like a Bushman taking a cocoon from its covering. Khuana had to do something. The ostrich stuck his long neck through the entrance and made three quick deadly jabs with his beak, almost striking Khuana's stomach. She had to do something quickly!

Her bow lay on the floor of the small cave. Khuana reached for it and searched for her poisoned arrow. The cave ceiling was low. She tried to stand up to get a good view of the ostrich through one of the holes, but this time the beak struck from behind, knocking her to the cave floor. She lay there stunned, while the bird reached in with its beak and tried to pull her out of her shelter by her skirt. She felt herself sliding toward the opening in the rocks and she braced her feet against the rocks to stop herself from being yanked out of her hiding place. She waited until the giant bird let go of her skirt, then she jerked it back into the cave. She quickly ran back to her place against the farthest rock. Panting with fright and exertion, she tied her skirt closer around her waist so there was no longer a flap for the bird to catch hold of. Her head buzzed. It felt like a cracked tsama melon. She put her hand in her hair and when she looked her fingers were bloody. She was lucky the ostrich had had no chance to strike with its toes.

The ostrich was still there. She heard its angry hissing and saw the heavy, deadly beak flashing in through the

doorway one moment and in through other holes the next.

She found her bow again and pulled it toward her with her foot. She almost panicked when she failed to see the poisoned arrow. She searched frantically, the sand clinging to the blood on her fingers, her broken hair-beads falling around her face. Finally she found the arrow, half covered with sand, and pulled it out.

When she looked up again a new and terrible fear struck her. The entrance to the cave was darkened. All the light from that direction was cut off, as if someone was trying to come into the cave. She was afraid to move. What if the ostrich tried to squeeze inside and got stuck in the entrance and couldn't get out? Khuana would never be able to push the heavy body away. She would be trapped inside.

She scrambled nearer to have a look. There was plenty of room for her to crawl out, but the giant bird had sat down with his back to the entrance. He was waiting for her to come out and he would catch her.

Khuana knew she must use her last arrow and she could not afford to miss. At the least sound she made, the ostrich turned its head to stare in at her. As she fitted the arrow into the bow, the ostrich saw her and quickly jumped to its feet, probing its beak into the entrance of the cave. Khuana quickly lay on the floor, took careful aim, and let the arrow fly with all her strength. It hit the bird in the chest, low, between the two long legs, and hung there like a long, damaged feather, but it didn't seem to bother the ostrich at all. The ostrich curved its neck and tried to pull out the arrow. After several tries, the loose reed came away leaving the poisoned arrowhead sticking in the bird's chest. The ostrich became frantic in its effort to get at Khuana. It pecked time and again into the cave, giving loud calls. It then ran half crazed around the rocks, trying to find another entrance, or trying to squeeze itself into the cave in order to get at her.

Khuana felt overjoyed that her arrow had struck the bird, but now she began to wonder if the arrow would kill the ostrich. Had she put on enough poison? Did the arrow enter the flesh or merely become entangled in the feathers? It was soon plain that either the poison or the sting of the arrow was beginning to have some effect on the ostrich. The bird ran around in circles and ran again around the rocks. Then there was silence. Khuana wanted to leave the cave to see what had happened to the ostrich, but she was afraid to move. She lay in her corner, her back pressed hard against the farthest wall, expecting to feel its beak on her head or foot, or to be pulled out of the cave, pecked senseless, and left there upon the open sand as a bloody mess while the ostrich rolled away its eggs.

After a time when none of this happened, she grew brave. Maybe the ostrich already lay dead from poison? She inched away from her position and moved nearer the entrance. Looking out, she was surprised to see the ostrich running along the floor of the valley. It ran deep into the valley and after disappearing for nearly a minute, came back towards her. She retreated back for shelter, but before it got anywhere near the cave it turned in a big circle as though its destination had changed and its one desire was to find its mate. But suddenly its movements became wobbly, and it ran about in a mad detour, making smaller and smaller circles, raising its useless wings to steady the clumsy body, looking every minute as if it would take off in flight.

Khuana crawled through the cave door and stood up amazed. She slapped her thigh with delight. Her arrow had done its job! The poison had worked! The ostrich was dying!

The ostrich, apparently in pain, turned suddenly as if it had just remembered Khuana in the cave. It ran as fast as it could toward where she stood, its long neck pointing the deadly beak forward like a spear.

Khuana stood rooted to the spot, unable to move as the ostrich came toward her. While it was still thirty yards away she thought she heard the snakelike hissing escaping through its beak. She was directly in the path of the giant bird and it seemed she would be crushed. She turned at last to run, looking over her shoulder. But unexpectedly, the ostrich's legs flew out behind him kicking up sand, and he slid forward to the ground on his chest, cutting a small furrow in the sand, forcing the beak into a small sand pile. It lay still. The ostrich was dead.

Khuana, about five yards away, stood spellbound for a time before she realized that it was all over. Her first action was to jump straight up and yell: "Grandmother, Morro, grandmother! We've got it! We've got an ostrich. Morro! Morro!"

But, then, something Khuana had never expected happened: she heard a loud roar from another direction and looked up to see the female ostrich running toward her. Khuana headed away and ran as fast as she could for the high rocks near their camp. The female ostrich let out terrible cries and roars that set the rocks echoing and sent jarring fear through Khuana. She thought the ostrich would catch her, but the bird stopped by the fallen male.

Khuana's grandmother joined her on the rocks and they both watched the female roar and hiss all the afternoon. Khuana was very much afraid. They clung to the rocks until the ostrich's voice stopped and she slowly walked across the flat space to her nest, back to the remaining eggs.

"She won't move from those eggs again until they hatch," said Gaushe.

12

Desert Laughter

Khuana and her grandmother dried and packed most of the ostrich meat. First they moved their camp near to the dead bird. Then old Gaushe was busy for the next three days, curing the skin of the ostrich and making it into two big karosses. While she was doing this, Khuana sliced and dried strips of meat in the sun and over the fire that she kept burning. Khuana and Gaushe had already decided they would stay there until Gaushe's leg was healed and they were fully rested and had enough food to go on to Guatscha pan.

Old Gaushe's leg was almost completely healed by the time they set out loaded with water, ostrich meat, and eggs. With two ostrich eggshells full of water and plenty of dried and baked ostrich meat, Khuana and her grandmother set out for Guatscha pan. It was a good trip across open desert—for old Gaushe's leg was now healed and they traveled through country she knew well. They walked at night and in early morning, stopping to rest during the hottest part of the day. It was one of the best times Khuana had ever spent. She learned much from old Gaushe about how a girl should dress and what she should wear at all stages of her life. On the fourth morning of their walk they came upon some dried bushes and grasses. Old Gaushe stopped and said:

"Now I am going to make you the envy of the other girls."

Gaushe bent down and picked a handful of grass seed and handed it to Khuana.

"Smell it."

Khuana did and a wide smile cracked her face. "It smells like a dream. It's like the ones we gave Nsue."

"Put it in your kaross. It's Sjaae, but of a different variety," Gaushe explained. Khuana had heard of the name and knew it was one of the nicest smelling powders, much prized and sought by many Bushmen women.

"How do I use it? How is powder made from it?"

"First you must grind it up. I'll give you my powder box made from tortoiseshell decorated with painted seeds. You can hang it from your neck and when you want to you can powder your face with a soft square of chamois skin. My box is in your mother's kaross. I put it there when I knew they were going to leave me."

"Now I can give back Nsue's powder box. Oh grandmother, you are so good to me." Khuana hugged her.

The next morning, tired and weary, they walked into the desert near Guatscha pan. It was Khuana's father, Kwi, who saw them first. He was returning to camp with his bow over his shoulders after an unsuccessful early morning hunt when he caught sight of them. He stared at them with disbelief for a while, then ran to meet them.

113

He took their karosses of meat and eggs and greeted them again and again:

"Morro! Is it you? My mother and my daughter?"

By the time they reached the clearing and the water hole, the early morning food gatherers were returning from all directions, having been told by small running children that some people lost in the desert had been found.

Nsue came running out from her mother's skerm and hung on Khuana's neck. Children picked at the karosses held by Kwi.

"Oh, Nsue, we found Sjaae grass of another kind."

"For powder, oh, Khuana you have all the fun."

Khuana's mother made old Gaushe sit down and at once looked at the healed wound on her leg.

"A miracle," she said. "Nothing but a miracle."

"Khuana, they're saying you shot an ostrich. Did you shoot an ostrich?" called Gishay. "I see father has ostrich meat and ostrich eggs in your kaross."

"Nonsense, Gishay, you know girls don't hunt," said his mother.

Gishay mimicked her. "Nonsense, Gishay." Then he added: "You don't know Khuana!"

Nsue said aside to Khuana: "Here comes old Mrs. Samgau!"

She came up shaking her head from side to side: "Gaushe, Gaushe! You went well? Morro? I felt sure you had joined Samgau and the others."

"I would have, but Khuana . . . " said Gaushe.

"Of course, the girl . . . I know it's the girl. She's too strong for death," said Mrs. Samgau.

114

Old Gaushe launched into a long story about their trip across the desert. She told them how Khuana had found a rabbit for them to eat and how they had found the salt pool and the fresh water with so many animal tracks.

"I said so," old Mrs. Samgau snorted loudly, "I told everyone, 'We haven't seen the last of them. That girl will beat the desert yet.' Didn't I?" she said, looking around. "I said, 'she will bring Gaushe here.'"

"They have ostrich meat," said Kwi, holding up the kaross with the strips of dried meat. "There's enough for everybody."

That night they made a feast in the camp, and danced the moon dance, even though there was no moon to welcome back Gaushe and Khuana. Everyone in the camp, young and old, brought small gifts and laid them at the feet of old Gaushe. She was the lucky one. She had conquered the desert. No old person left in the desert before had ever been known to come back alive. Gaushe had begun cutting ostrich eggshell for a beaded necklace to hold Khuana's ostrich eggshell canteen. Old Mrs. Samgau had promised to make the eggshell canteen for Khuana.

Old Tsona, Kwi, and the other men were very happy; they felt no longer limited to Guatscha pan. If they wanted to, they could leave and make their own camp at the other water holes, but in the meantime there was no hurry and it was pleasant enough to relax among relatives.

It amazed everyone that Gaushe and a girl had conquered the desert and now sat among them. But it did not amaze Khuana or Gaushe. They loved all of their family, relatives, and even other groups they met, but between them there was the love of a grandmother and granddaughter that was unselfish and for them it was enough. It had conquered the desert.

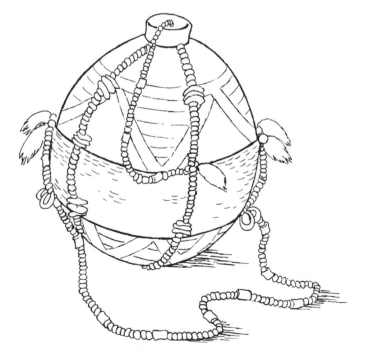

Glossary

Burrow—hole in the ground made by Bushmen to protect themselves from the sun during the day

Chamois skin—skin of a deer

Gao Na—God of the Bushmen

Gemsbok—a kind of deer

Guashi—musical instrument with strings

Infata Bush—a desert shrub; its scented leaves are used by Bushmen women

Jerboa—a small animal somewhat like a rabbit

Kaross—a leather cape of cured antelope or other kinds of skin worn by Bushmen women

Klipspringer—a small antelope that usually lives on rocky hillsides

Marula Tree—a short tree having hard bark and well adapted to conditions of drought; underneath this are found poisonous beetles

Omuramba—a dried-out riverbed; the river exists only during exceptionally heavy rains

Pan—(as in Guatscha pan) a flat salt area

117

Pupa—form taken by an insect during second stage of its life when it becomes a grub inside a small shell

Quiver—container for carrying arrows

Sanguaro—a type of cactus growing to giant size

Sjaae—a desert grass having scented leaves and flowers used by Bushmen women as a powder on their bodies

Skerm—Bushman hut; a shelter of branches stuck in the ground, bent together, and covered over with grass

Springbok—a kind of deer

Tracks—(of people/animals)—marks left by animals or people on the ground where they have walked

Tsama Melon—desert melon, usually green and white; it stores much water and is eaten by Bushmen during the dry season

Werf—A Bushman camp

MOSES L. HOWARD (Musa Nagenda), until recently a teacher in Kampala, Uganda, has taught at Ntare School, Uganda Technical College, and Kyambogo T.T.C. He has studied in England and the United States and has traveled widely in Africa. Mr. Howard is, at present, living in Tacoma, Washington. His first novel, *Dogs of Fear,* written under the name Musa Nagenda, has been published with much acclaim.

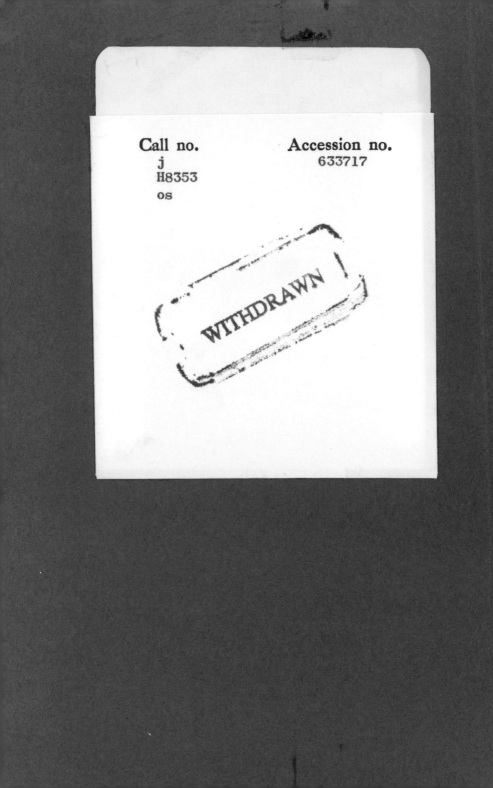